# My Heart's Desire

## June Masters Bacher

**HARVEST H̶̶PUBLISHERS**
Eugene, ̶gon 97402

*To*
*Son Bryce and His Wife, Sun,*
*My "Tar Babies"!*

**MY HEART'S DESIRE**

Copyright © 1986 by Harvest House Publishers
Eugene, Oregon 97402

ISBN 0-89081-521-6

**Printed in the United States of America.**

## *Other memorable books by June Masters Bacher*

The continuing story of Rachel Buchanan and Colby Lord along the Frontier Trail to Oregon.

Book 1   *Journey To Love*
Book 2   *Dreams Beyond Tomorrow*
Book 3   *Seasons of Love*
Book 4   **My Heart's Desire**

An adventurous saga of the American frontier and a young woman's quest to find a new beginning.

Book 1   *Love Is a Gentle Stranger*
Book 2   *Love's Silent Song*
Book 3   *Diary of a Loving Heart*
Book 4   *Love Leads Home*

*Quiet Moments*—A Daily Devotional for Women

# Contents

# Preface

Come with us now for one last glimpse of Oregon as it used to be. MY HEART'S DESIRE is the fourth and last of the newest pioneer series. Preceding it, with the same characters, were JOURNEY TO LOVE, DREAMS BEYOND TOMORROW, and SEASONS OF LOVE.

May you, like Colby and Rachel Lord, Buck Jones and Yolanda Lee, find that peace and joy can triumph over adversity. For God's ways, as mysterious as those of the rivers and mountains He created, can make life into a beautiful love story fulfilling each heart's desire.

Perhaps this story could have happened nowhere else. For settings influence the people who laugh, weep, live, and die—to live again—in them. And Oregon is the land where the storms will pass, the snow will melt, the clouds will drift away. Even so, the warmth of the love of our Lord, as revealed in the promises of His Son, will bring forth a never-ending spring.

That secret of love is My Heart's Desire for you!

—June Masters Bacher

*Commit thy way unto the Lord;*
*trust also in Him,*
*and He shall bring it to pass.*
—Psalm 37:5

# 1

## Wedding Day

It was the trill of sleepy birds that awakened Rachel. For a moment she lay motionless, listening to the sweet music of spring as her dreams receded back into the night. A new day was at hand—a special day, the birds seemed to be saying. Then came the familiar ache of loneliness...mixed with something else...a sense of dread. Only she was not going to think about it. Not yet.

Spring had come back. The winter had passed safely. Ahead lay the warm months of planting, blossoming, and the sweet fruition of harvest. Brisk winds had blown the clouds over the mountains and melted the last of the snow. The white skeletons that winter had made of the trees now flushed green against the darker green of the Oregon mountains. It was a time of miracles for the valley folk...when cows brought home new calves, sheep bleated in the higher meadows, and ground was ready for plowing. And another miracle was due today...

For weeks now the women of the village and surrounding settlement had busied themselves with the upcoming wedding. Time was marked more by the event than by calendars or clocks. The O'Gradys' cabin was ready for a roof-raising. But it could wait until after Yolanda's wedding to Brother Timothy. Land sakes, the two had waited long enough. First it was Colby Lord's sudden return to the village he had financed—a time for rejoicing indeed,

considering how he had been held prisoner by those out-
laws who would have tortured and murdered everybody
in Lordsburg to learn the secrets of Superstition Mountain.

"What them what don't know the Lord will do for a little
filthy lucre!" Aunt Em had muttered uneasily as she
recounted the eggs she was saving for the wedding cake.

Then there had been another delay in naming the date
which would unite Rachel's lifelong friend in marriage to
Timothy Norval. First, folks had to decide about priorities:
Homes for all so they could prove up on the homesteads?
Building Lordsburg according to the dream which had
brought the biggest wagon train ever over the Applegate
Trail from the East? What about digging deeper into the
pockets of Superstition Mountain? It was unlikely that a
single seam of gold would hold that mountain together. And
it was everybody's problem, since Cole (bless him!) had seen
fit to record all as owning a share. Best pray about it all.
The Lord knew their needs. But the answer was long in
coming . . . and best postpone the wedding.

Rachel had been overjoyed when the decision favored
going on with the building. Blue Bucket Mine could wait,
but the families needed roofs over their heads, houses they
could call their own instead of the makeshift quarters they
had occupied so patiently in the horseshoe of buildings
which became places of business as the settlers vacated.
Now Cole could be at home, where a husband and father
belonged.

And Yolanda could be married!

Between the shadows of sleep and the fingers of morning
which tried to lift her eyelids, Rachel remembered that it
was Yolanda herself who created obstacles later.

"Life is so uncertain for a beginning minister," she had
said in answer to Rachel's *why*.

"All the more reason you should be living it—that is, if
you are sure you love Timothy. *Are* you, Yolanda?"

"Of course!" Yolanda had sounded sincere. "As soon as we can file a claim for a homestead, and we know for sure that Timothy's calling keeps him here—not that I wouldn't go somewhere else with him—" Yolanda added hastily. "But I want him to be sure—"

"About serving here or marrying you?"

Yolanda's face flushed. "Maybe," she said slowly, "it's wise to let a friendship grow slowly into love."

"Two years?"

"How long did it take *you*, Rachel? You never did tell me about that whirlwind courtship of yours."

It was Rachel's turn to color. She felt the hot flow of blood rise to her face, then recede, leaving her pale and shaken as always when mention was made of her marriage. The ugly circumstances were the one secret she had kept from Yolanda. Maybe, since Yolanda was on the verge of taking her vows, she had a right to know. What better gift could she, as matron-of-honor (if Yolanda ever made up her mind), give the bride than letting her know that there were a million kinds of love? That the beginning, good or bad, might not determine the success of marriage? Waiting as Yolanda was doing might be as big a risk as her own impetuous leap...

"Rachel!" Yolanda prompted.

"I don't know where to begin—" Rachel remembered having sat down on the corner of Yolanda's iron bedstead, the mattress so neatly tucked beneath a nine-patch quilt with its bright scraps of calico mingling with more somber gingham.

"We never worry with words," Yolanda had reminded her as she pushed aside a bolt of princess satin that her mother had sacrificed her egg money for, then sat down beside Rachel.

"Well, you remember my father's distaste for work—his only ambition being to marry me off to any man, no matter how unprincipled, who could keep the cellar stocked with rum—"

When Rachel's voice trembled and the words caught in her throat, Yolanda put a supporting arm around her. Yes, she remembered.

End-on-end Rachel's thoughts tumbled back, and she was able to go on with the story. It was as if the years between had never been. There was no color and adventure in her life that the perilous journey over the Oregon Trail had brought. There was no husband with whom she was madly in love . . . no ethereal, autumn-leaf daughter that Providence had provided . . . no dimpled toddler conceived in love . . . no *now*.

There was only the bleak, shadowy house in the eastern fishing village and her father's rage. Until Cole . . .

Even now, her eyes snapped with indignation at the ugly memories of the arrogant men that Templeton Buchanan brought to inspect her. At least now she was able to smile at mistaking Cole for one of them—tall, bronze, beautiful Cole. As beautiful in spirit as in flesh. A man she could respect.

"It was you who brought us here, you know," Rachel said.

"I?" Yolanda's naturally red lips made a capital O.

"Remember the letters about the Garden-of-Eden beauty of the Oregon Country? 'Not a place of man's creation,' you said, with its crystal-clear waters and leafy bowers, 'a beautiful place for a townsite'—and that was Cole's dream—"

"Well, wasn't I right? And it fulfilled your dream, too."

Yes, Cole—once she discovered that he had not come to appraise her at all but to collect a sizable loan from her drunken father—was a dream come true.

Even now, Rachel had to but close her eyes and behind their lids see and feel the wonder of her runaway marriage. Unaware of the stranger's wealth, but convinced of his honor, she had allowed herself to be swept up to ride through the Atlantic fog of early morning. Astride the great black stallion they galloped away—winds loosening her long hair, lifting the long skirt like ship sails on a storm-tossed sea, and pushing her slender body against the strong chest behind her. How impossible . . . how exciting . . . how *wonderful*!

"I was afraid my father would follow, as he threatened—" Rachel paused, realizing that her experience would certainly be no argument against a growing time for love. Yolanda, usually the more talkative of the two, had remained silent. And when Rachel turned to look at her, she saw great tears well up and spill from Yolanda's usually laughing, Mediterranean-blue eyes.

"Oh, darling, I have upset you!" Rachel opened her arms and Yolanda fell into them, sobbing openly.

"It's not that—it's that I—I want—I want and almost had what you have, dear Rachel. And I lost it. *I lost it!*"

Julius Doogan! What was the good in reminding Yolanda of his betrayal of the wagon train, his brutal retaliation against Cole, his false promises to Yolanda? She knew. And yet her heart was unable to accept. In holding onto an empty dream, the bright flame that once was Yolanda had dimmed and now threatened to go out. Rachel was determined not to allow that to happen to her treasured friend.

"Time heals," Rachel soothed, instead of blurting out the blunt truths as she once would have. "Memories fade."

"In two years?"

Rachel laughed. "Touche!" she said.

But Yolanda had made up her mind that day. And since then, as far as she could tell, Yolanda was content with the decision. Something of the old Yolanda was missing, but Rachel had become convinced that if this marriage were God's will, He would supply the missing ingredient . . .

● ● ●

Rachel came back to the present when she heard the excited squeal of a child. Mary Cole! Then, remembering that Star (a regular little mother to the two-year-old now that she had turned eight) always took the baby out to swing on Saturday mornings when there were no classroom duties for her, Rachel, or Yolanda.

Yolanda! Now she knew what the birds were trying to tell her. This was Yolanda's wedding day!

"I should have told Cole to call me when his alarm clock rang," she said aloud as she hurriedly scrambled for a robe. But today Cole had business too. The company of Chinese workmen would arrive and need Cole's directions to the mine.

That accounted for her feeling of dread. Opening the mine meant more loneliness and . . . but she could get no farther with her thinking. "Please, Lord, remove this sense of premonition."

# 2

## Happy the Bride...

Streamers of sunlight wound through the crimson wash of azaleas growing low on the hillsides surrounding the village. But in spite of the brilliant sunlight, Rachel took note of the dark plush of clouds gathering around the higher peaks. There was, she thought as she hurried to the Meeting House (where the wedding was to take place), the sniff of rain in the air. If only she could take hold of those bright streamers and use them instead of the sateen ribbons to mark the pews! A bride must have sunshine.

Yolanda herself interrupted Rachel's thinking, "Happy the bride the sun shines on!" She called out gaily.

Before Rachel could answer, Agnes Grant appeared out of nowhere. Her shrill warning cut through the festive air: "Get inside—get inside *now*, afore he sees you! You know it's bad luck should th' groom be seein' th' bride. And we've been havin' bad luck a-plenty without you addin' to it. *Go!*"

Aunt Em, her wide girth wrapped in a Mother Hubbard apron, appeared in the doorway of the hotel to save the moment.

"Aggie! 'Tis you who's to be gettin' inside. Y'left without finishin' your job. Only one layer's frosted and there's 11 t'go on this cake!"

Mrs. Grant cast a spiteful look at the two younger women. Then, head down—as if her hawkish nose were pulled earthward by gravity—she stalked toward the hotel.

"What if—I mean—she scares me." Yolanda's voice had lost its gaiety. "*Should* I go back to my room?"

"Not until we've had one last look. Enjoy it, Yolanda. You'll be too excited this afternoon. And," Rachel inhaled deeply, "as for Agnes Grant, she's a natural-born troublemaker. Remember all the problems she caused on the trail? I told you about that. And you know how she has stirred up trouble here. Promise you'll ignore her?"

Yolanda bit her lower lip, attempted a smile, then nodded a definitive yes.

Together the two of them headed for the Meeting House. As they walked, Rachel surveyed the changes around them. The original horseshoe-shape of the growing village had enlarged to a circle, the hollow of a giant cup, with the mountains rising in a great protective green saucer around it. Cole had worked so hard. And of course this was only a city in its infancy. One day it would enlarge to fit inside his dream. She wished again that he could have followed that dream without the interruption of Blue Bucket Mine. But others had their dreams, too.

Chairs were scattered everywhere on the grassy slope, now referred to as the "Village Green," the hub of Lordsburg. Refreshments, laid out in everybody's best china, covered the tables, which the men had erected hastily of rough timbers and the womenfolk had draped with snowy bedsheets—starched, ironed, and lavender-scented. The tables dripped with honeysuckle, its pungent odor mingling with the strong coffee, grape juice, and freshly baked pastries that added sweetness to the pine-scented breeze. Thoughtfully, the men (well-acquainted with the unpredictability of April in spite of the forecast in *Poor Richard's Almanac*) had erected a canopy of stitched-together canvas and arched it above the tables.

"If she rains, we gonna be prepared," Brother Davey said with a degree of pride. Aunt Em cast him a withering glance and, with a yank at his side-whiskers, the onetime circuit rider amended, " 'Course now, th' good Lord ain't a-gonna be sendin' no rain, there bein' no red sails in the mornin'—that bein' Bible!"

"Pa's still insisting on singing," Yolanda said as Rachel reached for the latch to the Meeting House. "I told him he couldn't—his job being to give the bride away. He said I was too valuable to *give* away anyhow—meaning—oh, Rachel, I shouldn't have said that."

"It's all right, Yolanda. You know the story. It would be about like your playing your own wedding march." Both girls laughed, then Rachel asked if Aunt Em still insisted on trying to play. Yes, Yolanda said—even though the only music she could coax from the harpsichord was "Battle Hymn of the Republic" and that always set the *whole* congregation singing...

Rachel was unaware that she had stood at the door hesitating while Yolanda talked—unaware, too, when Yolanda's voice trailed into silence. Then Yolanda gave a light laugh. "One would think *you* were the bride!"

Rachel tried to brush her silence aside. "I *was* thinking of my wedding," she said, which was true in part. But something she had seen troubled her. At the far end of the village, opposite the hotel that Brother Davey and Aunt Em managed, a little grove of manzanita—its branches gnarled together like witch's hands—almost obscured a tent which had not been there yesterday. A fortune-telling tent!

Cole and Buck (the city's manager) as well as the City Council had guarded against businesses which fed on the weaknesses of the flesh. They had said yes to the forthcoming newspaper, even though newsprint and a printing press must be shipped from back East, but no to the saloon and gambling houses, no matter how much revenue the dough-faced man with currents for eyes promised. It was yes to the livery stable but no to the brothel, where ladies of the night would "accommodate" trappers, miners, and other wayfaring strangers.

It was Brother Davey who had turned back the gaudily decorated wagon laden with scantily clad girls, since the mine had been in operation and the other men were away.

How then had the men let the tent get by unnoticed? Rachel felt a strange sense of foreboding, but she was not going to let a shadow cross Yolanda's day. All the while she pondered the tent's presence, she had been yanking at the latch of the Meeting House door. Somebody must have locked the door from the inside.

And then the door burst open. "Surprise!" all of Rachel and Yolanda's pupils called out at once.

Both Rachel and Yolanda gasped in delight. Surprise indeed! All the rough benches used for desks on weekdays had been arranged into pews and covered with sheets. Somebody had spread with a faded green carpet the aisle that Yolanda would walk down to meet her future husband. And the rest might have been the setting for a fairy tale. Sunlight poured from the windows to bathe the altar, which was entwined with wild roses. Great baskets of daffodils and yellow tulips from Aunt Em's garden, themselves looking like bottled sunlight, mingled with the purple wood hyacinths, making the room a bouquet.

Yolanda was the first to speak, "Oh, children, it's beautiful!"

Rachel, seeing Star advancing (one nut-brown little hand clasping the baby hand of Mary Cole and the other filled with dogwood) felt a surge of emotion. It no longer mattered that the new church was unfinished for the wedding. This was just fine.

Fine, yes, for neither girl knew that the day would change their lives forever.

# 3

# Black Curse

Judson and Nola Lee, Yolanda's parents, had moved their dozen children and few belongings (brought into the village while the men were mining the mountain) back to their cabin in the "back country." Yolanda, however, had taken Aunt Em's advice and occupied a room at the hotel until the wedding.

"We want everything accordin' to your likin' now, Dearie," Aunt Em said to Yolanda. Yolanda had put up no argument. Strange that nobody ever did. Knowing that the woman had a lump of gold for a heart (having no family of her own, the good woman adopted them all as her "spiritual children" along the trail), the village folk were guided by her homespun wisdom.

It was in the small hotel room that Yolanda had hung her wedding dress, so lovingly stitched by fingers made nimble by a lifetime of quilting. "Every bit as fashionable as those fancy ones in *Godey's Lady Book*," Nola said with justifiable pride. The shimmering satin gown was simple, designed to let the bride outshine the dress itself. The demurely-high neckline ended with a French lace-ruffling which cupped Yolanda's face like petals around a fragile blossom. The wide, full sleeves did what they were designed to do—made the bride into an auburn-haired angel, Rachel thought when Yolanda tried to stand still for her mother to measure the hem of the five-yard sweep of floor-length skirt.

"Have a look at that waist!" Aunt Em had said in awe. "Nothing but an ant could fit into that!"

Carefully wrapped in a sheet, the dress now hung on the wall alongside the soft lawn nightgown, its allover lace topper, and the navy-blue suit, bag, and shoes that Yolanda would "go away" in—all a part of Rachel and Cole's wedding gift. "A *trouseau!*" Yolanda had breathed. "I just never dreamed—but it is I who should furnish it—" at which point Rachel had interrupted, "I know, I know. But you and I were never ones to put the law above love! Maybe I never told you that Cole bought my clothes. I escaped with only what I had on my back—and it was threadbare—"

Then both girls turned away, each to hide her tears from the other. But the pretext was to look at the other gifts.

The featherbed was one that Aunt Em had made—"Had to rob my last gander of his feathers t'get it fat enough with down to call goosehair," she had said, smoothing the striped ticking. "He's still in hidin', that gander. Talk about a *woman's* vanity!"

Other women had provided canned and dried fruit. And more was still coming. Enough, Judson said, to fill the ark.

Now Rachel and Yolanda took one last look to make sure the three petticoats were laid out and Yolanda's small bag was packed for the three-day stay in Salem. All was in order, Rachel assured the now-nervous bride as she checked her list. Yes, the red roses were picked while the dew was on and were now in the rain barrel until time for the fern to be added and the bouquet finished with the sateen streamers. Callie, the Lees' youngest, knew exactly how to scatter the petals, and Star was well-coached in how to carry the white Bible that Cole had ordered and to remember to lift her pink skirt as she stepped up to hand the Book to Brother Davey—little Mary Cole following with the ring. Brother Davey would do fine, Rachel assured her. The words were printed in large letters and flour-pasted to the pulpit lest he got carried away and decided to preach a sermon. Now, to do her hair.

"I'll roll it on rags for you, then you get some rest!" Rachel ordered. "And stay away from that fortune-telling tent."

The words were out before Rachel realized she was going to say them. All morning she had thought of that place, undoubtedly set up by Agnes Grant, who had said over and over that any wedding was doomed until both bride and groom knew the will of the stars. And now Rachel's wandering mind had betrayed her. Yolanda's eyes had enlarged in fear and her face was ashen. "You mean—"

"I mean *stay away*—or do I have to lock you inside?"

Yolanda had promised, but Rachel felt uneasy as she returned to her quarters. It had been a full morning. Quickly she peeled the last of the winter's potatoes for soup, laced it with cubes of ham, then set it to boil for the children's lunch. That should tide them over until refreshment time at the midafternoon wedding.

Now she sank wearily down on the bed beside the window, where the early-afternoon sun slanted through the trumpet vine to dance across the worn carpet. It would be nice when the big house was finished. Nice, but not essential to happiness. She, Cole, and their daughters had been happy here. Certainly she agreed with Cole that cabins for the other settlers were more important. In fact, she would miss the little rose garden and the lilacs which had grown to giant trees and now at the peak of their bloom scented the air. She must remember to gather an armful for another table in case the neighbors, as they likely would, brought a basket dinner for a surprise celebration after the wedding.

Feeling drowsy, Rachel shaded her eyes with the palm of one hand and glanced up at the towering peak that was Superstition Mountain. More barren than most, it was still beautiful in its own way. Right now the sun reflected on the glittering granite soil, making it into a mountain of gold. Maybe this was the mountain Cole told her fitted into the Indian lore—that of the "shining mountain above the Great River that leads to the Southern Sea." If so, it was to be left undisturbed. . .a home of their ancestors' "long sleep". . . not to be mined. . .

Moving her free hand idly, Rachel saw the hundred facets reflected in the sunlight from the enormous diamond on her left hand. She looked dreamily at the rainbow hues in her husband's mother's wedding ring, no longer feeling guilty. It was a thing of beauty—not unto itself so much as what it represented. A circle of unending love—and Cole's pledge to it.

The sun slipped behind the buildup of white clouds and the room was full of shadows. Weren't the clouds edged with rickrack of darkness? Rachel could not be sure, because her eyes were heavy. And then she must have dozed.

She awakened with a start. Somewhere below there was a scream of fury—a scream that could belong only to one woman: Agnes! Rachel was on her feet immediately and, wiping the sleep from her eyes, she forced them to focus on the scene before her. Cole, her Cole who was always so gentle and mild-mannered, was ripping the makeshift tent apart and kicking at the collection of demonic tools that Mrs. Grant had assembled. . .tarot cards. . .a glass ball. . .a Ouija board. . .and what appeared to be a human skull.

Rachel had never seen Cole so angry before. Yet his voice was low and controlled. "You told me you were giving all this up when I allowed you to join the wagon train."

The gaunt-framed woman, who had begun preparing herself for fortune-telling by winding her head with a dingy, red headscarf, raised fiery eyes to Cole. "I am not ashamed of my Gypsy background—not one whit—"

"Nor need you be, Mrs. Grant. But you should be ashamed of your behavior now. The skull you have looks suspiciously

Indian. Do you realize what that would cause if any one of the tribes discovered it? And, as for your ungodly practices of behaving like the Witch of Endor, I won't have it. Do I make myself clear?"

Agnes Grant flinched before Cole's steady gaze. Maybe it was the firm set of his jaw that caused her to lower her head. But she was not one to give up without making sure she had wounded another.

"Who's t'say there cain't be no tradition—"

"Clean up this mess and return that basket of silver to its owners! Do it *now*! Sometimes I wonder if the practice of burning witches at the stake wasn't a good idea—"

With a startled cry, Agnes Grant cowered and began to gather the remains. Even as she worked, however, she continued to mutter. "Your high-and-mighty wife *dreams*—"

"Keep working! And let me remind you that you're to speak of my wife with respect. She is Mrs. Lord." Cole paused and looked up at the window where Rachel stood. There was no time for her to turn away from what she was sure he did not wish her to see and hear. Would he drive the woman away? She deserved it. Still, she was a widow—

"I will jot down some passages in the Bible I want you to read—and, yes, that is an order too. We'll begin with Exodus 22:18, and then there are about three more verses forbidding the satanic practice of witchcraft before we get into Revelation...remember, read all of these!"

Mrs. Grant was still bent over picking up the remains when Cole turned away and strode toward Rachel. Another moment and his long legs would bring him running lightly up the rough outside stairs leading to their quarters.

But not before Mrs. Grant called out raucously, "I s'pose I ain't good enough to be attendin' the weddin'—"

"It's not a matter of your worthiness. The Lees have included the entire valley, and you are among us."

"Well, I'll be there—and I'm tellin' you I looked into the

future a'ready . . . and they's a black curse on this weddin'. You'll see—"

Cole did not answer. And his step on the stairs was heavy.

When he entered the door, Rachel held back the questions she wanted to ask. She simply rushed into his arms instead. There, with her head buried against the warmth and security of his chest, all questions and apprehensions simply melted away. "Oh, Cole, I love you so much—"

Her voice was muffled by the chiming of a clock. Rachel felt Cole look up to check the time before he whispered, "Rumor has it I'm in love with you, too—and I've an idea I want to share after the ceremony, a plan."

"About the mine?" Rachel was afraid to move.

"The mine's in full swing. Thanks—strangely enough— to one Julius Doogan. He brought the hordes of Chinese workmen here with a railroad scam . . . but for now I'd like to see the church."

Rachel let go reluctantly. As she turned for her shawl, she thought she saw a movement in the manzanita thicket.

# 4

## Rehearsal

"The guests are arriving already!" Rachel glanced in amazement as she and Cole hurried the short distance from their quarters to the Meeting House.

"You know, Rachel," Cole said, tucking her slender hand in the curve of his arm, "there will never be another place like this again—the bearing, caring, sharing. I have so much to thank you for."

Rachel squeezed his arm. "Thank the Lord instead!"

Yes, this wide valley was indeed special—chosen, really, just as those who peopled it. A land where God balanced the seasons just right to seal in the seed with winter snow. Then, come spring, He always sent the sun to warm the watered earth. And each spring, as in this beautiful April, legions of green sprouts would line up to stretch, strengthen, and arm themselves against the enemies of weather and insects. Then winter was forgotten. The valley's people were much the same. They were inspired to marshal themselves against all odds.

Rachel paused to savor the moment. As far as the eye could see there were fields of green climbing the lower hills. Crops, good crops. And beyond the cultivated hills stood the mountains of virgin timber to keep the mills going. It would be a good year, just as the *Almanac* predicted, winter having yielded its tyrannical rule early. Chinook winds had melted the snow in February to overflow in the river in the low-lying lands, only to recede to add power to the current, which would keep the mill wheels turning. It was easy to fancy all the hibernating animals yawning before abandoning their dark refuges. All pointed toward prosperity here—unless too many men joined in the mining. Maybe with the Chinese here...

"Cole, it's going to be a good year—I just feel it—"

Cole glanced at her sideways in surprise. "Of course it is, Darling—but what's troubling you?"

"I was wishing—oh, Cole, *must* you continue with the mine? I mean, the crops are so promising, and the village is becoming a city—"

"What if the crops fail?" His question was gentle but spoken as if his mind were made up. "We must repay the loans, you know—and the families here are entitled to the profit I all but guaranteed." Cole hesitated, then—reaching a decision—continued, "I wasn't going to go into this, but I know for sure there's more gold—after this morning. Lots of it."

"Did something happen?"

They had paused in front of the Meeting House.

"It's on the other side, too—the section I filed claim for before. There's a bed of strangely colored dirt there near the stream. I dug into it and found a yellowish gravel—only it isn't gravel at all. When I washed it through the riddle, I knew for sure—"

"Gold—gold nuggets."

A look into his face told the answer. There was that expression of excitement she had come to recognize and hate—yet love at the same time.

"Enough," he whispered, leaning close to her ear, "to pay off all the loans and allow the men to repay me so I can keep my shipping business going—for all of you here. I wanted you to know in case...Rachel, I have a lawyer who would take care of everything—*Rachel?*"

But she had turned away. *Don't think. Just look. There, see Elsa O'Grady unloading her special black crust bread from the wagon? Concentrate on the elderberry jam that Liz Farnall is sure to have in that basket . . . the pies . . . the thick slices of sugar-cured ham . . . DON'T THINK!*

"You wanted to see the inside," Rachel said quickly, hoping to hide the tears in her voice. "We'll have to hurry—"

Inside, the Meeting House (which today would reach its peak of glory—Lordsburg's first wedding) had taken on the pale yellow glow of the afternoon sun. Its air was now heady with flowers. And momentarily Rachel felt a sense of unreality. Even before he spoke she knew her husband had brought her here for a purpose.

She was right.

Cole extended his right arm. "We're going to rehearse— you and I."

"But—it's Yolanda and Tim's wedding—"

Cole's soft laugh echoed somewhere near the pulpit. "The bride never rehearses, remember? Give me your arm."

As if in a sweet dream, Rachel placed her left arm over Cole's, her fingertips touching his. Both of them glanced at the beautiful diamond whose light seemed to fill the dim room with little prisms of light. She had never loved Cole more. Neither had she ever felt closer to God. "I am the light of the world," His Son had said. And Rachel felt that the all-knowing God used many mediums as reminders.

"You never had the chance all brides should have, the experience of walking down the aisle." Cole's voice was choked with emotion.

Rachel felt tears of joy cloud her eyes. This was a moment to cherish—made up more of holiness than worldly delight. Somehow it seemed in keeping as there came softly, but distinctly—as if from a long way off—the sad-sweet wail of a violin. *Violin?* Her wide eyes questioned Cole's.

"Old Mr. Solomon fiddling on the roof," Cole whispered in the sanctity of the moment. "Tradition he brought from Israel."

Rachel's tears spilled as slowly she and Cole moved to the altar. "I, Colby Lord..." Cole began. And together they renewed their sacred vows while the fiddler on the roof played on and on the tunes that were as old as love.

"I will repeat these vows at the wedding, saying them again in my heart. Then, surprise! Back to the leaning inn where we consummated our marriage—oh, Rachel, I love you!"

# 5

## Unfinished Song

It was a radiant Rachel who hurried down the stairs and toward the hotel. Just wait until Yolanda heard that she too was going away on a honeymoon! Not in style, like the buggy that Timothy had rented for his bride, but riding a wildly snorting stallion under the dark of the moon!

The sun had now started downward and was slanting through the buildup of clouds around Superstition Mountain. Rachel even smiled a little, remembering Aunt Em's telling Star and Mary Cole that the sun, when its parallel fingers reached through the clouds, was "drawing water" from the river for the "upstairs well." Soon it would be emptied on earth below. Maybe the omen even portended rain. In Rachel's state of euphoria it could flood and she would ride through it as she had done on her wedding night!

She found Yolanda in much the same mood. Yolanda, so tall, slender, and regal in the satin gown, was still fussing with her already-perfectly-braided hair which encircled her head like a glowing halo. She had chosen to wear no train, saying it was a little *too* fancy and might embarrass the guests. True, Rachel had said, and had delighted Yolanda's mother by agreeing with her that the off-the-face cap with the short wisp of rose-point veil she had worn when she married Judson would be just right.

"Oh, Yolanda, you look beautiful!" Rachel breathed as

Yolanda handed her the cap for adjusting over her braids.

The big bell, salvaged from a mission after an Indian raid, began to toll in invitation—the echo of its iron clapper bouncing against the mountains and into the surrounding valleys. There had been some debate as to how many times the bell should ring. Ten times meant worship services. Eight meant "water bell" for the children during recesses. All who failed to take a last gulp from the granite dipper would have to show good reason for dipping the long-handled gourd dipper into the pail in back of the classroom. A single bell meant "Line up!" Valley folk were happiest when the bell rang on and on, spelling out good news. As for bad news . . . well, nobody was going to think about that today.

There was a poignant moment when the two lifelong friends embraced, each holding back the tears that trembled along her lashes. The difference was that suddenly Yolanda trembled.

"You understand, don't you, Rachel? I mean—I need to be loved. It isn't true what they say, is it—I mean about love's being to man a thing apart while it is woman's sole existence?"

"Sayings, except for the Lord's Word, are one man's opinion—in that case, Byron. And he came along a long time after God decided Adam needed a wife! Now, let's not miss your wedding."

The bell had stopped tolling. And from the Meeting House came the muted notes of "The Battle Hymn." "Aunt Em must be using the soft pedal," Rachel whispered, and was rewarded by Yolanda's smile.

The wail of the fiddle softened, its minor key of an ancient lamentation blending with the answering strain of the harpsichord inside the Meeting House. Rachel lifted her own skirt with one hand and Yolanda's with the other as the two hurried quickly across the freshly sickled velvet of the Village Green.

There was a bad moment at the door just before it swung open to admit them. In that fractional second Rachel, thinking Yolanda's tug at her arm was a case of last-minute jitters, whispered, "Everything will be fine—"

"No, no, it *won't!*" There was desperation, near-hysteria, in Yolanda's hoarse whisper. *"Look!"*

Rachel's eyes darted quickly to follow the direction that Yolanda's shaking finger pointed. And there, almost hidden in the hutlike grove of manzanita, was the skull that Agnes Grant had had in her tent this afternoon. Grotesquely, it was mounted on a stake, and beneath it were two crossbones. The kiss of death!

Rachel's heart turned over in horror. Then, to her relief, the great, red-whiskered bulk of Yolanda's Scotch-Irish father blocked the doorway. His blue eyes looked almost angry, so determined was he to control the emotional quiver of his chin. He stepped aside to let Rachel pass.

Brother Davey, looking a little like a starved penguin in his oversized frock-tail coat and stiff-bosomed white shirt, had positioned himself at the altar. Beside him stood a white-faced Timothy Norval. He looked younger than his 27 years—vulnerable somehow, open to hurt. But her eyes shifted without further thought to meet the eyes of the best man. Her husband. Her lover. But today her "groom."

*This is our real marriage. . . not a wedding. . . a marriage. From which holy state have come two beautiful children. Oh, heavenly Father, I thank You. . .*

For one shining moment of promise their eyes met. Then, with pride, they turned to watch their elfin Star approach the altar, white Bible in hand, dark eyes carefully lowered to the floor. Behind her came a wee, golden-haired fairy escaped from beneath a toadstool umbrella—little Mary Cole, balancing the ring on the blue velvet cushion as she toddled between the pews. *Every child*, Rachel thought, *inspires its parents*...

Aunt Em, her hair crimped for the first time Rachel remembered, glanced over her shoulder from the crude wooden bench—hidden by her ample body. Catching sight of the bride entering on her father's arm, she lifted her foot from the "soft" pedal and placed it on "loud." A fusillade of jubilant notes attacked the rafters. At the signal, the great crowd stood, their voices rising to join the music:

> In the beauty of the lilies
> Christ was born across the sea,
> With a glory in His bosom
> That transfigures you and me;
> As He died to make men holy,
> Let us die to make men free,
> While God is marching on.

The bride was at the altar. Her father was handing her to her husband-to-be. The audience sat down, reserving the triumphant chorus for the recessional—little knowing it was to be an unfinished song.

# 6

~~~~~

# Explosion of Horror

The sacred vows were exchanged. Timothy slipped a simple gold band on Yolanda's finger.

"By power invested in me—"

"*Vested*, Davey Love," Aunt Em prompted in a stage whisper.

"...vested in me, I now pronounce you man 'n wife!"

The young minister brushed his bride's cheek with a shy kiss. But something had gone wrong. Emmaline Galloway's plump hands, raised in preparation for the "Glory, glory..." chorus never came down on the keys. There was a rumble of thunder, followed by a fervent ringing of the great bell. It was too soon. Abe, Rachel's oldest brother, was stationed at the door and ready to give his younger brother the signal. Only he had given none. Instead, ashen-faced, he stood watching in terrible fascination as the bell swung back and forth, back and forth, in the unmistakable rhythm of a dirge.

The wedding ceremony took place at four o'clock. Now and in the hours to follow all was blurred forever in Rachel's mind. She was aware of a rushing from the Meeting House, while the aged fiddler on the roof played on...

The world had grown dark, the sky above it an inverted caldron of boiling clouds. Tongues of flame leaped from cloud to cloud, followed by earthshaking thunder—

At least, that was Rachel's first impression. She was never

33

quite sure just when she separated the snarling fury of a storm from the terrible explosion that was in progress. Even when Abe screamed "The mine!" she felt great drops of rain against her face and mindlessly saw the circles which the raindrops made on her "going away" dress. . .

"I told you, I *told* you! It ain't like y'warn't warned!" Agnes Grant was screaming in the midst of the confusion.

But for once Aunt Em made no effort to stop the hysterical woman. She was rushing toward Buck, who was ringing the bell—*Buck*! That was the first time Rachel realized he had not been at the wedding. Cole must have shared his plans with Buck, and Buck, ever the faithful friend, decided it was he who should supervise the Chinese workmen.

Now Cole was at her side, but she could only see him through the haze of shock that was fogging her vision.

"It's the mine, Rachel. Rachel!" Cole was shaking her gently. "Rachel, Darling, are you all right?"

Rachel raised her stricken eyes to his and then let them go past along the trail so often traveled to Superstition Mountain. . .up, up, up to the top, where smoked spewed out furiously and the rim of the crater was aflame.

"The workmen—the workmen—" she gasped.

"They're trapped—inside the tunnel—"

"What tunnel, Cole? You never told me—" Rachel tried to lick her dry lips but found the effort too much. "But, then, you never told me much about the mine."

That was unfair. The truth was, she thought—closing her eyes against the fork of lightning that split the inky vault overhead—that she had not wanted to hear. These things, and more, she longed to say to Cole. But the time had passed. This was *now*. Both of them were needed.

Trying to fight off the blackness that begged to wrap itself snugly around her, Rachel gasped for a breath of air. "Oh, Cole, where are they? I mean, Yolanda—Tim—*everybody*?"

But one glance told her that some of the guests were

leaving. Hurriedly, men helped their families into the wagons while calling out, "Be right back, Cole, soon as the wife 'n young'uns is settled in . . ."

Yes, of course. The men must go to the mine. But *Cole*? Hardly aware of moving, she tightened her grasp. And just as quickly, she let go. "Tim—" she whispered.

"Gone, Darling—he went first. His calling is to minister. And so is mine—in a different way." He was removing her arms gently. "Try to understand—"

*Try*? She *was* trying. And so was Yolanda. *Yolanda*!

"This is their wedding day."

"You must go to her—" Cole's voice trembled. "And I must go to Buck—"

But Buck had come to them. He placed a sun-bronzed arm around their shoulders, concern showing in his earth-tone eyes. Fatigue showed in every line of his face and, for the moment, he looked older than his 30 years. Rachel reached out a compassionate hand and touched his sleeve.

Buck covered her hand with his enormous, work-worn one. He even managed a crooked smile. But his eyes were on the mountain.

"We'll need the log chains—block and tackle—and, of course, all the manpower we can get . . . picks . . . shovels . . ."

Most of the women were gone, and the few remaining men were already assembling what they hoped would be rescue tools. Rachel let go of her husband's hand. He was right . . . she must go to Yolanda. Aunt Em would know where to find her.

"Are they alive—or do you know if there's hope?" Rachel heard Cole ask. But she did not hear Buck's reply.

She started toward the hotel and then turned. Cole was coming toward her. "Give me a kiss, Sweetheart, and promise not to worry."

"I can't do that," she said, holding back the tears. "We'll

be back together soon. *I promise that*," Cole whispered.

*Yes, either on this earth or in the world to come . . .* but the words remained unspoken. She was being crushed to her husband's heart. And then, in a sudden downpour of rain, he was gone.

Fighting her way toward the hotel, tears blending with the rain, Rachel saw that the grinning skeleton was gone.

# 7

## The Long, Long Trail

Yolanda was lying facedown on her bed when Rachel found her. Her mother was trying to unwind the veil from its coil around her wet head and soothe her in the only way she knew how, crooning softly as she had done when her firstborn was a baby.

Nola Lee looked up when Rachel entered. "What's there to say?" She asked with a piteous shake of her head.

"If you would like to go help Aunt Em make coffee—" Mrs. Lee nodded gratefully. "If she needs me—"

When the door closed behind Yolanda's mother, Rachel knelt beside Yolanda. "Remember what we always did in times like these?" When Yolanda only nodded with a little moan, Rachel went on, using a command she hoped would restore Yolanda to reality, "*Say* it! What did we do in a crisis?"

"Prayed." The word was a little moan into Yolanda's pillow.

"Then pray now. Pray as you have never prayed before..."

A short while later the two girls, dressed in raingear, were astride "Tombstone." They would have to ride double, Yolanda explained, the men having taken all other horses.

"Yes, Cole took Hannibal," Rachel answered, remembering her last glimpse of the black stallion as he reared and neighed wildly before horse and rider were swallowed by the gaping mouth of the stormy night. "And *your* husband took the bay mare."

Yolanda urged the aged animal forward. Then, turning from her position in front, she said something over her shoulder. The whistle of the wind all but carried the words away. But Rachel caught a phrase: "... *husband*—what a beautiful word..."

At the bottom of Superstition Mountain, Yolanda pulled Tombstone to a stop. "He'd know his way," she said slowly, "being no more blind at night than in broad daylight—but now?"

Rachel strained her eyes but was blinded by a flash of lightning that seemed to explode over their heads. But even behind closed eyelids she had seen enough to know that the way was blocked. Trees lay across the old trail at a crazy angle and there was a plateau of mud where the narrow trail used to be.

Thunder rumbled, causing the very earth to tremble.

"I'm blinded," Rachel ventured to break the tension.

"And I'm deaf—but, wait, there's another way up. We'll have to take it. There's no choice."

The old horse, uncertain of gait at best, picked his way slowly up the muddy, unfamiliar trail. Often he stumbled, causing the two riders to fight for balance. Rachel felt a familiar sense of unreality stealing over her. What were they doing, two young girls out here alone? No, they were not impetuous young girls anymore. They were women. *Pioneer* women. And, as such, they were going to stand beside the men they loved. But even as she redefined their position, some demonic thought rose from the grave of the night to mock, "*Widows*—young *widows* on the long, long trail to futility—"

She cried out against the thought and was glad that the howling wind sucked away the sound. Yolanda needed her. Cole needed her. The children—

Then, suddenly, the brooding mountains seemed to poke at the rain-darkened sky, releasing a deluge that blinded the eye and made further travel impossible. Yolanda tugged at the rope that served as a rein, pulling the faltering steed toward what appeared to be a grove. But a flash of lightning revealed a tepee shape of sapling poles over a pit with a pipe in the center.

"An Indian hut?" Rachel whispered when there was a momentary lull of the wind.

"No—it's an old Mexican camp—only I didn't know it was here. They must have tunneled in from this side, using a mule and an *arrastra*—" The wind sucked away her voice.

The word was unfamiliar. But Cole had said something about a tunnel. Maybe they were closer to the mine than they realized.

She was never able to share the thought with Yolanda, because at that moment the entire world lighted up in a red-orange flame such as neither of them had ever seen before. Above their very heads, it seemed, was a circle of fire . . . its burning breath upon their faces. Rachel felt the fiery fists of the flame squeeze her heart, rendering her helpless. Her very bones were molten, her mouth as dry as the ashes that fell around them.

Then came the explosion that could well have split the world in half. Tombstone reared wildly, pitching both riders to the ground. Then, with a pitiful whinny, he panicked and ran stumbling down the rugged mountainside.

Dazed by the fall, Rachel's head felt detached from her body, her mind no longer in command. She attempted to struggle to her feet, but her clothing made her a prisoner, wound around the branches of fallen trees. If only she could move her legs. If only her brain would command its members.

And Yolanda! Where was Yolanda? Rachel called out again

and again. When there was no answer, she began to recite passages from the Scriptures which were of most comfort: " 'He shall give His angels charge over you, to keep you in all your ways.' *Do you hear, Yolanda?* Say Isaiah 41:10 with me: 'Fear not, for I am with you.' *Yolanda!*"

Now a hush covered the earth. A deadly hush. There was only the fiery smoke and a sort of eerie twilight created by the blazing inferno that once was the peak of Superstition Mountain. And against that deadly glow was the staggering silhouette of Yolanda.

Rachel understood. The top had blown off the mountain, reducing what was once the highest peak overlooking the settlement to a lower level of evil-eyed coals. And beneath them...*oh, dear God, no!*

With herculean strength she somehow managed to rise uncertainly to one elbow. Using it as a lever, Rachel pushed herself to her feet. Dispassionately she heard her clothing tear. Now she was nearly nude and shaken with cold, but she did not care. All that mattered was getting to Cole.

Forcing herself to move forward—slipping, sliding, and falling—she prayed over and over, "Give me strength, Lord—just give me strength to climb this hill."

Even as she prayed, she felt dark phantoms surrounding her, faceless apparitions clawing at her flesh. "Widow—widow," they leered. But she pushed on.

So single-minded were the two women in search of their mates that neither saw the long line of dark figures: men, their neighbors, and their friends—heads lowered—moving single-file down the original trail. Neither did they hear the muted voices chanting, "Amazing grace! how sweet the sound..."

A funeral procession. But the only sound Rachel heard was the heartbreaking cry of a coyote in its perpetual search for food. And then Yolanda's scream.

# 8

## To Bury the Dead

For less than a second Rachel was consumed by fear. Its tendrils coiled around her heart, shutting off the blood flow, rendering her body helpless. And then it attacked her throat, stripping away whatever voice remained.

Later she realized that the Lord must have sent a guardian angel to breathe new life into her motionless body, to hand her a morsel of courage from the bottomless hamper of blessings—and then with gentle hands to erase the horrors of memory forever because it would be too much to bear.

Yes, it had to happen that way—else how could she have moved so dangerously near the roaring furnace—so near that she could feel the flames reach out to singe the ends of her hair—to snatch Yolanda back just in time? Oh, praise the Lord for rain! Had both she and Yolanda not been soaked to the skin, surely they would have perished.

Instinctively she placed her own body over Yolanda's. For one frightening instant Yolanda fought her, then her body went limp in Rachel's arms. And together the two of them lay moaning in the bed of oozing clay while fire raged over their heads.

Rachel felt herself drifting in and out of consciousness. One moment she was aware of trying to lift her weighted body up and make one last struggle to save herself and Yolanda. The next she was overwhelmed by a false sense of well-being—an "it-makes-no difference" world which required no struggle. Just surrender. And death.

It became increasingly hard to tell when she was semi-conscious or when she was hallucinating—whether she actually saw the grinning skull floating above her scorching eyes, sweating bodies of painted Indians advancing, then retreating, their war cries driving arrows through her pounding forehead. Surely she was not imagining the one familiar face... *familiar*, but who? Somewhere inside her, wild laughter churned—laughter she was too weakened to express. She had recognized the face of the man... and, of course, he would not help her...

And then sleep would no longer be denied. Through its smothering black robes, Rachel was unable to hear the distant voice that called her name. And, had she heard, she would have been too far into the uncharted netherworld to respond...

"Here they are... oh, thank God! Men, this way with the blankets—we've found them. Rachel... Yolanda... *wake up*! Maybe they're alive... I'm not sure! Hurry with the lantern.... *Hurry!*"

Rachel felt a hand slide beneath her neck gently. *The settlers had come to bury their dead... her, Cole, Yolanda, Tim... and on their wedding day...*

# 9

## Saved! For What?

In a beautiful dream Cole was bending over her. "Rachel, darling Rachel! Wake up—wake up!"

Wake up? Why, when his lips were brushing against her forehead, his arms cradling her as gently as if she were a very special child?

But he was spoiling it all with his insistence. "Speak to me, Rachel, speak! Oh, Rachel, let me know you are all right—" His voice shook with emotion. Oh, how wonderful to be loved by such a man! She smiled a little and drew a deep breath of contentment.

Then she realized something had gone wrong with the beautiful dream. Her lungs refused the air and she choked, gagged, and came to with a shudder of mind, soul, and body.

"Dear God in heaven, I thank you..."

The words were right. But the voice was not that of her husband.

"Cole! *Cole*—" The words she tried to scream were but a whisper. And she could get no further than the name. Recognition had come. The man who held her was Buck Jones.

"Easy does it—easy." Buck's soothing voice reached Rachel from a million light years away.

There was a supporting hand at her back, another holding her head up ever so slightly. "Drink this."

Having no will to resist, Rachel allowed Buck to pry open her mouth with something hard and metallic. A spoon. A spoon holding hot liquid. Rachel could not swallow, and the scalding contents trickled down her chin and onto her neck. She wished she could feel the pain. But there was nothing. Her flesh was without nerve endings.

"Drink it, Rachel!" Buck's voice was forceful, as was the push of the tin cup to her rigid lips.

And then she caught the welcome aroma of coffee. Sweet, thoughtful Buck remembered what she and Yolanda had forgotten . . . coffee . . . and Cole would be needing something bracing and hot.

*Hot*! No, fire was hot. Cole needed a cool, refreshing glass of spring water. Maybe Buck had that, too . . .

"Drain the cup, Rachel." Rachel obliged.

Buck laid her down gently, then tucked a dry blanket around her. "The men are bringing a litter for transporting you and Yolanda down. Sorry it took so long," he went on as he blotted her wet hair with his handkerchief, "but we had a tough time finding you—"

"We took the back trail," Rachel said faintly, pleased with herself that a thread of memory remained.

Expertly Buck felt for her pulse, then with a shy apology began to test her fingers one-by-one, bend her elbows, trace the bones in her legs. Poor Buck . . . how embarrassing for him . . .

"Nothing broken there. Does your neck hurt—or your back?"

"Nothing hurts."

"Thank God for that—"

"So everything is all right—" Rachel felt a certain detachment, a dangerous lassitude. Buck had made no reply, but it did not matter.

Rachel was vaguely aware of lights dancing like fireflies. Lanterns? Yes, men swinging lanterns, for she could hear their voices. And they had brought the litter, put together hastily of parallel poles, secured by rawhide strips, and topped with worn canvas.

Buck lifted her as if she were a fluff of thistledown. And she was being rocked back and forth like a bird's nest in a summer breeze. She would rest now.

But rest was impossible with Buck telling her to stay awake—his voice pleading, commanding, then pleading again. All the way down he kept up a flow of talk. Star and Mary Cole were drinking their fill of grape juice...left over, you know...Aunt Em was showing them how to make a cat's-paw from twine...did Rachel know how?

His voice was a lullaby. And a male chorus was answering ...bass...tenor..."No trace—yes, I saw it happen...no way to get to them—either of them...workmen? Only the Lord knew how many..."

Only they didn't know. Buck should tell them all was well. Until she heard Yolanda's scream: "*Saved*? For what?"

# 10

## Awakening

The next 12 hours were only impressionistic paintings in Rachel's mind, the colors washing together without clear representation. Faces appeared, then blurred. Aunt Em bending over her, forcing broth between her clenched teeth. Cole—no, Buck—kneeling to pray. Crowds milling in confusion . . .

Gradually the visionary sense gave way to distant sounds. Children laughing, only to be shushed by their elders. Sighs of the tireless wind . . . a meadowlark wheeling overhead, calling to let the world know he was in command. So the universe must be continuing according to spring's command. Then the louder, shriller whistle of the *Oregon*, as the flatbottom boat wheezed downriver . . . pause . . . the sound of men's voices as they prepared their poles for manning the log ferry to meet the boat and unload the goods that Cole had ordered. So the river must be high. Yes, the rains would have swollen it. Just once did Rachel open her eyes. And then only because it seemed somehow necessary that she verify her assumptions. Through half-closed lids she saw the murky rivulets of water coursing sluggishly through the unpaved streets.

When Rachel awoke the morning of the second day, her mind was clear. She knew her name was Rachel Buchanan Lord. That she was 23 years old. And that today, unless she had miscalculated, was Monday. It was only the immediate past that was blurred and fragmented.

Without trying to move her body, Rachel turned her head toward the window. She realized then for the first time that she was in the hotel instead of her own quarters. There was a reason, and it would return at her bidding. But for now she pushed it back. There would be a way—there *had* to be a way—that she could face it.

Outside the window one dewdrop clung to the tip of a pine needle. Trembling, as if afraid to let go, the tiny droplet caught the glory of the April sunrise. Strange how a single drop of water could reflect the whole world while an ocean could not!

Fascinated, Rachel watched. Would the dewdrop surrender its life to plunge downward, giving life to others? It would be but false victory to hang there, allowing the warm rays of the sun to sweep its vapor upward—only to let it fall when the clouds bumped against the mountains. Either way it would fulfill its destiny of watering the earth.

How like life. How much of it did one control? And if there were choices, would the decisions lead to the same end by another route? If she and Cole—

*Oh, Cole! My Darling, my Darling.* But, even as her heart cried out, Rachel knew there would be no answer. She knew, too, that she must manage to get up, face this day, and all the empty years ahead, without him.

"Rachel?" The whisper was Buck's from the corner of the room, where he must have kept an all-night vigil.

"Oh, Buck—it's you—" Rachel's voice trailed off before she was able to finish the words of appreciation.

"Lie still. Aunt Em will be in to help with a—uh—she'll help you prepare. Then I'll bring our breakfast."

Aunt Em must have been standing just outside the door because she was there immediately. Without a word she brought a steaming basin of water, a cake of yellow soap, and a soft flannel cloth. Quickly, as if she had a schedule to keep and was running late, the great woman's sun-and-wind-weathered hand sponged Rachel's aching body as gently as if she were a baby being ushered into the world.

Then, with a tight squeeze of Rachel's hand, Aunt Em said practically, "Davey's poached you two eggs'n made coffee that'll dissolve th' spoon. Now, eat it all—hear? Oh, dearie—" with a broken sob the motherly woman bustled from the room.

Buck entered with the tray. Setting it on a small table beside Rachel, he leaned over and propped her head up by means of a second pillow. Without asking if she could feed herself, he began buttering the sourdough biscuits, breaking them into bite sizes, and pushing them into her mouth.

The food was sawdust to Rachel's dry tongue. But the coffee was hot and bracing. Buck, who had not spoken during the meal, took the empty cup when she had drained it.

"How did it happen, Buck? How did he go?" There was no expression in her voice and little feeling in her heart. Something—or was it all?—of her had died with him.

"Rachel, not now—this can wait until you're stronger."

Rachel suddenly clawed at his hand. Why must he always try to protect her? "*Tell me!*"

Buck ignored the angry red marks that her fingernails had made as they dug in with a sort of fury. Inhaling deeply, he took both her hands in his large ones.

"I have no idea how much you remember. I didn't even know you were there—and neither did Cole—"

"What caused the explosion? Or *was* it an explosion?"

"God alone knows," he groaned. "Maybe gas from the mine, or a volcano, or a bolt of lightning, or a cave-in from the storm, or nitro or gunpowder—"

"You mean it could have been man-made? But *who*—why—?"

Buck's eyes darkened with despair. "We can't rule that out, but chances are great that we'll never know. It could even have been something else—oh, Rachel, would to God that I could have died for him—"

Something burned at the edges of Rachel's memory, blessedly deafening her ears to Buck's words. "Indians—" she said slowly, reaching back into the darkness of faint images, fantasies, and inventions of her mind. "Indians—and a skull? A face—the face of a man—I'm sure I saw somebody who could have helped...and didn't—"

*No, no, that made no sense. But nothing did. And, besides, neither she nor Buck had come to the point.*

Still bound by the unfeeling chains of shock, Rachel looked directly into Buck's eyes. "How did it happen with Cole?" Her voice was flat and lifeless. But her words would tell Buck that she knew. She only needed to know *how*.

Buck sucked in his breath so sharply that there seemed to be no air left in the room. "None of us were there in time to caution Tim. He was unacquainted with the dangers—and it wouldn't have made any difference in his determination to get to the dying workmen...to pray over them. A man of God could never ignore their cries. I've searched my soul for an answer..."

He needed comfort—comfort she was unable to give. His voice faltered, and for a moment silence engulfed them. Then Rachel managed to push open the door of her mind.

"Cole?" she whispered hoarsely. "He tried—"

"—to get to Tim, yes—and I wasn't there—I should have been there. I saw and I knew, but try and believe me, Rachel, when I tell you I wasn't close enough. That will haunt me for the rest of my life—"

Desperately Rachel tried to weigh the whole structure of horrible events. But she was in the gray area of a strange limbo—understanding and yet not understanding at all—where all decisions are impossible to make. Who was she to pass judgment? She should have been there herself. She was his wife.

"Go on," she said flatly, showing no regard for his remorse.

Buck looked away, his face wretched. "The fire was raging out of control. But there was one moment when I thought Cole might make it. I think he reached the upper level where Tim was standing just above where the others were trapped. By the time I could get there the beams collapsed. The smoke was so thick...but I could see his hand...and I tried—I tried to reach his hand. I tried—"

Rachel was no longer listening. She was seeing herself in the same situation. *Reaching...tearing...screaming...* and finally managing to pull Yolanda back. Yolanda, who did not want to live. Wasn't that what she said as the men transported the two of them down the mountainside? And Cole who *did.* Oh, it was unfair, unjust, and cruel.

Then came a wild desire to hurt as she had been hurt. And she was beating Buck against his chest, oblivious to his own tears searing her hands. *"Cry,* Darling—" Buck choked.

# 11

## Yolanda

Ignoring Aunt Em's protests, Rachel insisted on seeing Yolanda. After her fury had spent itself, Rachel herself found a certain mindless courage to go through the motions of adjusting to her loss—at least on the surface. Inwardly she was hanging by a thread—a thread which she hoped the Lord would strengthen. Only prayer could sustain her.

Pulling a daisy-printed dress over her braided hair, she examined herself in the mirror. She was surprised to see that her face looked unchanged except for the haunting expression in her hazel eyes. The green was gone from them. With determined fingers she pulled the corners of her mouth into a smile before meeting the children, after which she would call on Yolanda.

"Mother Mine?" The little silver-spoon ring of Star's voice raised in question surprised Rachel. She had not heard the door open. Quickly she turned, and, seeing that Star held Mary Cole's baby hand, she opened her arms and gathered the two precious daughters to her breast. They were her reason for going on—her daughters and her husband's dream.

"*Que triste*," Star whispered against Rachel's cheek.

Yes, how sad. How sad for her, for the children, and for all the settlers who depended on Cole for their entire future. He was the cornerstone of Lordsburg. And her life.

"We must be brave," Rachel found herself saying with only a faint tremor in her voice. "Daddy would have stayed with us if he could—"

"I know," Star answered with a composure beyond her years; "God needed him."

"Wan' my daddy—*need* him!" The lisping words were a sob from little Mary Cole. And, although she clung to Rachel's neck until the dimpled arms almost stifled her, it was easy to see that she was not to be comforted.

"Sh-h-h!" Star's thin brown finger went to her mouth in an effort to silence the baby. "*Madre Mia's* tired." Then her great, brown eyes—dark pools of appeal—focused on Rachel. "We'll see him again one day, won't we, Mother mine?"

"Of course, my darling...of course!" The words were wrenched from Rachel's dry throat while her heart was crying out, *Why, Lord, why, why? They're so young and trusting. WHY?*

"See Daddy now. *Need* Daddy!" Mary Cole's innocent eyes were wide with hope.

"We can't for awhile," Star said gently. "Not until Mother Mine finishes her work here. *Verdad?*"

The Spanish was dwindling from Star's conversation since the time Rachel had felt the little waif's tug at her skirt on the wagon trail and taken her to her heart. But, under stress, fragments of her native vocabulary returned—a little trait which always betrayed what her solemn face concealed. Now it tugged at Rachel's heart. And, swallowing hard, she heard herself repeating, "Yes, *verdad*—it is *true.*"

Rachel felt that she would have been unable to maintain her composure much longer had there not been a sharp whistle from below. It was Buck's signal to the children. He had found a bright feather, made a willow whistle, or seen a strange animal track. Buck—dear, wonderful Buck— her husband's best friend, who would always be around to comfort the widows and the orphans...

• • •

Yolanda was still at the hotel, Aunt Em said. That, and the funeral tones which Rachel heard at the door of the room where such a few days ago the bride-to-be had prepared for her wedding, caused Rachel to pause before she knocked. Yolanda had not sent for her and, for the first time, she wondered why. Suddenly she was concerned. Something was wrong—something which caused a prickle of fear to creep along her spine.

Her fears were well-founded. The moment Nola Lee opened the door, Rachel knew. She raised questioning eyes to the stricken face of Yolanda's mother, and there she saw the answer.

"She rambles," Mrs. Lee whispered brokenly. "If anybody gets through to her, it will have to be you—oh, sweet Rachel, I'm so sorry—so sorry about *your* loss—"

Rachel murmured an automatic *Thank you* and brushed past to where Yolanda sat cross-legged on the bed, the wasted bouquet cradled to the bosom of her wedding dress. Something clicked in Rachel's mind. Yolanda was shunning the present. Unable to accept the reality of Tim's death, she shut out all other reality as well. For her time stood still. The dress told the story.

"Yolanda!" Rachel spoke sharply, hoping to draw the sightless eyes in her direction.

Yolanda turned toward her but continued her rocking. Worse, there was no recognition in the colorless face. And her great blue eyes were those of a sleepwalker.

"The wedding's at four—need help—Tim's waiting . . . waiting somewhere that I can't go—need help—"

Rachel knelt beside her, feeling the cords thicken in her own neck as she held back the hysterical sobs so near the surface. "I know, darling—I know. But the wedding's over—maybe in your excitement you forgot?"

For one hopeful moment Yolanda stopped her rocking. Then she resumed as her eyes stared blankly into space.

"Tim's waiting—have to go to him—"

"But not in your wedding dress, darling," Rachel pleaded. "Let's get you into something appropriate—oh, your going-away dress—"

There was no sign that Yolanda heard, but she submitted to being undressed. Quickly Rachel reached for the filmy nightgown which was still on its rack on the wall, and, with Mrs. Lee's help, coaxed Yolanda from the satin dress and slipped the night garment over her head.

"Now, you should rest awhile—remember? Close your eyes and I will stay with you."

Yolanda allowed herself to be lowered to a pillow, and her legs straightened. But her eyes remained open, set in their sockets like burnt-out stars.

"Would you mind leaving me alone with her?" Rachel asked. "Surely you could use a cup of Aunt Em's coffee—and a little rest."

"I'm glad you've come—" Nola Lee was moving noiselessly toward the door gratefully, but the cloud of anxiety lingered on her pale face. "Will she be all right—I mean—oh, Rachel, I couldn't bear it if—"

Rachel placed her arm around the woman who had been her own mother's only friend during the long years of her illness. "We must not borrow trouble—not yet. It's a terrible shock—almost too much to bear—"

At the door the quiet little woman paused. "But you—you bore up—you survived—" Nola ended with a little sob.

*My brain survived. My heart did not.*

"She needs time—love and prayer. That's the best we can offer, *all* of us. Why don't you have Brother Davey call a prayer meeting?"

Mrs. Lee looked at her strangely for a moment before replying. "We have, sweet Rachel—oh, how we've prayed for both of you! I keep forgetting that you too have been poorly."

When the door closed behind Mrs. Lee, Rachel went back to Yolanda. Maybe, through some miracle, the Lord would provide her an anchor, something to hold onto until she could come back to reality.

For over an hour Rachel tried to fan whatever spark of sanity might remain buried in Yolanda's tortured brain. Had she eaten? Was she sleeping? Had any of the school children been in to see her? The two of them must be getting back into the classroom...and "Oh, Yolanda, the new building's coming along. Soon Amity School will really have its own building—"

Nothing registered. And then Rachel took a long shot—long and dangerous. "I love you, Yolanda—even more than when we were little girls playing with corncob dolls. Remember back home the playhouse your father built for us?"

Yolanda lay as still as death. But something told Rachel she heard but would not respond. "One day you will have another house and you'll not need to make-believe a husband. He'll be there—you'll meet another man, love again—"

"Tim—Tim loves me—needs me—" Yolanda's voice was weak, her words almost incoherent.

Rachel breathed a prayer and then said flatly, "Tim is dead, Yolanda. Killed in the mine—with Cole—and—"

Yolanda screamed. Her eyes rolled back in their sockets and she jammed her fist into her mouth, biting until the blood ran down her wrist. "No, *no,* no!"

And then she lapsed into unconsciousness.

# 12

## A Letter Unread

Judson Lee, unable to express his grief over his daughter's condition other than in righteous anger, stomped in and out of the hotel sitting room shaking his fist earthward. "We'll gitcha—now ye be hearin' that, Satan! Get thee behind me and stay there—ye took our men but ye ain't taking me gal!"

Then he would go into his strange mixture of Scotch and Irish languages, banging his burly red head against the wall for emphasis. His wife did not cross him at such times, but Aunt Em stood up to him as she did to her husband. Men were like piecrust—had to be handled lightly.

"Behave yourself now, Judson, afore you get Yolanda more upset than she is—and send her over th' brink!"

Judson's eyes widened. "Ye be meanin' she—might—destroy herself? Ye be meanin' th' devil's done *that* much?"

"I mean," Aunt Em said patiently, "that my folk medicine ain't a'gonna bring the girl out of this. She needs a doctor and she needs 'im quick!"

Judson stomped one foot, headed toward the wall on this particular day, thought better of it, and came back to stand facing Aunt Em. The woman's medicine was designed to kill. But she had been known to show some horse sense.

"Ye be 'aving some body in mine? I mean, besides that traveling woman in men's pants who passes by once in a coon's age peddling her wares and making claim of some kind of license t'be practicing medicine? *Practicing*—bah!"

Their voices drifted off. Rachel, who sat beside Yolanda, wished Aunt Em could convince Mr. Lee. Yolanda was getting no better. In fact, she was losing ground. If she recognized any of her family or friends, she gave no indication. Mostly she slept away the hours with never a twitch of the face or a faint moan. So, even in her dreams, Yolanda determined to remain marooned on her island of self-exile of grief. Anything, *anything at all*, would be better than this, Rachel felt. If only Yolanda would respond, then the two of them could face their grief together. Maybe even conquer.

A short time after Judson Lee's conversation with Aunt Em, Rachel rose stiffly from the cane-bottom chair where she had sat beside Yolanda for an hour. She was about to leave when the reflection of the telegrapher's green sunshade flitted across the room, blinding her momentarily, then fading as quickly as it appeared. Willie was in a hurry.

Rachel stooped to peer beneath the green window shade, drawn against the light, and watched as the wiry little man knocked at her door, then, pushing his sleeve up higher and snapping it beneath the garter, he knocked again before she possibly could have responded.

Seeing the telegram in his hand, Rachel ran on tiptoe across the room, and—wincing at the squeak of the hinges—closed the door quickly. Once outside, she signaled William Mead to wait.

As usual, his colorless face was without expression. But his ink-stained fingers shook a bit when he handed the rough yellow paper to Rachel. The message must be important.

Quickly she scanned the telegram. Then she read it carefully to be sure she had absorbed the message. Frugal on words, it was long on content:

MY CONDOLENCES *STOP* MARSHALL HUNT & I ARRIV-
ING SATURDAY *STOP* BRINGING NOTED DOCTOR *STOP*
RESPECTFULLY GENERAL JOHN WILKES *STOP*

"Is there a reply, ma'am?"

Rachel hardly heard and was never sure she replied, so
eager was she to share the good news with Buck, Yolanda's
family, and the Galloways. All of them loved the General,
his width of gold-braided shoulders and military bearing
never failing to lend security. And one could say the same
for Marshal Hunt . . . poor man, Rachel hoped he had found
help for his wife, whose mind, like Yolanda's, had chosen
to hide inside herself. How like them both, Cole's staunch
allies, to think of a doctor. It would be a sad reunion, but
one bringing hope.

"Mrs. Lord?"

"Oh, I'm sorry, Willie—"

Even as she murmured the words, Rachel was moving
away. But not before the telegrapher had stuffed a fat
envelope into her hands—an envelope whose contents were
to once again change her life in the Oregon Country.

• • •

Buck looked up from where he, Star, and Mary Cole were
making frog houses by putting their bare feet into the damp
soil along the riverbank, patting it into shape, then carefully removing their feet. He smiled a little sheepishly and
reached for his boots.

"Aunt Em would say we'll all catch our 'death of
dampness'—Rachel, what is it? You're panting!"

Instantly Buck was on his feet. "Here," he said, spreading
his old woolen mackinaw and patting it in invitation. "Sit
down—"

"No, I—" Rachel had been about to say there was so much
to do and so little time. Then, glancing at the sun-speckled

ripples of the river and catching the heady aroma of sun-sucked resin from the trunks of the fir trees, she found herself dropping onto the seat he had prepared. For a fleeting moment the past dissolved. The four of them were simply enjoying a picnic, marking time until Cole returned from one of his countless business trips.

And then the moment was gone. It was too soon. The past was still an open, bleeding wound. Maybe it would never scar over.

The brightness of the day dimmed. And what she had come for receded in Rachel's mind.

"Oh, Buck, why should I be alive when Cole is dead? And why should I be of sound mind when Yolanda—" stifling a sob, Rachel forced herself to go on, "or is she the lucky one? Reality is cruel—maybe her world is kinder—"

Buck's arm was around her shoulders, drawing her close. "I know, Darling—believe me, I know!"

"You couldn't possibly know," Rachel objected, but she did not pull away from the protective circle of his arms. "You see, Buck, it may have been I who—pushed her into that insulated world where she could feel no pain—"

Her body convulsed by sobs, Rachel told him then how, in an effort to shock Yolanda back from that mindless world, she had told her that Tim had perished in the fire. Buck was so silent she thought he had not heard. And when he spoke, his voice was choked with emotion.

"No, Rachel, no, Darling. It wasn't you—you aren't to blame—unless you would blame me for not saving Cole?"

"No, Buck. No, I would never do that."

"Then we will have to accept what has happened and go on—trying to think of it all as a matter of timing. Maybe if the wedding had been earlier or later . . . or the Chinese workmen had not come that day. But if Cole had been there, he would never have permitted Tim inside that mine—any more than I would have allowed Cole—" Buck's voice faltered and he stopped.

Why was it that she always felt cleaner inside when she talked with Buck? There were so few friends like him and Yolanda. Rachel's mission came to mind then. But first she must ask one more question of Buck. Only he could remove the burden of secret guilt she had carried.

"The timing, Buck—do you think it could work the other way, too? That if I had been less hasty—held my peace, had more patience, whatever the phrase—that I could have spared Yolanda this, or maybe brought her out of it?"

"Nobody could have spared her, Rachel. Don't you see it is of her mind's choosing—something that even she cannot control? Something or somebody would have triggered it. Even left to her own resources, she would have snapped."

"Have I told you lately how much I count on you?" Rachel reached out and took his hand, squeezing tight.

"You'd better!" he teased, the words lighter than his voice.

But Rachel did not notice. She was reaching for the telegram, her mood suddenly lifting above the ashes of her loss.

"We need to talk, Rachel—"

"I know." Rachel was unfolding the yellow sheet for Buck to share. "The future—but not now. I can't plan yet. If you'll just take care of the business until I can get Yolanda ready to go back to the classroom with me—and a memorial service—"

*Memorial.* Oh, the pain of the word! So bathed in it was Rachel that she did not see the look of pain cross Buck's face. She handed him the telegram, then picked up the unread letter she had dropped.

# 13

## Dr. Killjoy

The ashes strewn over Lordsburg cleared away with the first brisk wind. But those in Rachel's heart remained. The light lingered longer in the cobalt sky . . . the hills brushed with feathery azaleas, then changed to a blaze of glory as the rhododendrons welcomed May. And still she had not found the courage to look up at what used to be the peak of Superstition Mountain.

Soon, she promised herself. And soon she would reopen school, too. *Soon?* After the memorial service, she supposed. The General, usually so careful about details, had not mentioned a date—only a day of the week. Two weeks slipped by before he arrived—two weeks of loneliness, pushing grief away as far as her mind would reach, of watching people come and go . . . trying to be kind . . . awkward in their attempts at trying to comfort her when they too were suffering.

Rachel did not mind postponing the memorial service. In a sense she was no more ready for it than Yolanda. What she did mind was the delay in medical attention for Yolanda.

The townspeople, glad to have something to help work off their frustration, rallied to clean away all debris of the explosion of the ill-fated Blue Bucket Mine. The final gesture was for the men to sweep the sun-dried streets while the womenfolk busied themselves kalsomining every room in the hostelry. The General was to occupy the "Blue Room" and Marshal Hunt the "Green Room"; and wasn't it wise to reserve the "Red Room" for the new doctor? Now, seeing that the pound apples were "bigger'n bird eggs," green-apple cobbler would be nice. There were a few hams left in the pork barrel, and the fryers were ready.

Rachel paid little attention other than to feel a deep gratitude. Most of her time was devoted to watching Yolanda, hoping and praying for a change. None came.

She was with Yolanda when the General, with his usual pomp, arrived—riding in front, Aunt Em reported, "like he was a'gonna take th' next hill." Behind him rode the Marshal and the young doctor in single file.

Rachel busied herself washing Yolanda's face and fluffing her hair about her once-beautiful face. The skin was drawn tightly across the sculpture of the cheekbones, as if some artist had peeled back a layer of flesh. The expressionless blue eyes were only half-open, giving Yolanda the look of a discarded china doll—one with an abundance of glorious hair. At least it had not lost its sheen, Rachel was pleased to note as she brushed it gently and let it fall about Yolanda's thin shoulders.

As she touched Yolanda's blue-veined wrists with sachet, Rachel suddenly became aware of another presence in the room. She felt rather than saw the figure behind her. She whirled, bumping into a stranger and causing his black bag to fall from his fingers.

"Oh, how clumsy of me—" Rachel murmured in confusion.

"Yes, wasn't it!"

This was the doctor? Yes, he had to be. Well, he lacked a lot in bedside manners. And then his keen eyes were looking straight into hers. For a moment Rachel was taken aback. Somehow she had expected an older man. But he was not new to the field of medicine, having treated Marshal Hunt's wife. All this Rachel was thinking as she backed away from the exceptionally tall man who showed signs of immense vitality and whose voice—well, yes, the baritone of it was more pleasant than the words it produced.

Well, it did not matter. Nothing mattered if he could help Yolanda.

"This is Yolanda, Dr.—?"

"Killjoy. Dr. Maynard Killjoy. You may leave the room."

His words were an order. An order Rachel obeyed. *Killjoy.* A perfect name for him.

# 14

## Another World

Rachel waited outside Yolanda's door. Some of her family should be here, but nobody had known when the doctor would come. In their absence, Rachel would fill in. Certainly it was improper for a man to be alone with a young lady, even though he *was* a doctor. And a very pompous one, too, unless she missed her guess. No matter what he did, said, or turned out to be, Rachel stored her original impression inside her brain for a future weapon, although just when she would need a weapon made little sense.

What seemed like hours later the doctor opened the door and came out, quietly closing the door behind him. He studied Rachel for a moment as if she were the patient before speaking.

"It's best that we leave her alone for awhile. I've given her a sleeping powder—"

"*Sleeping* powder!" Rachel gasped before she realized the words were coming. "All she has done is sleep since—"

A look of annoyance crossed his face. "This is different—experimental, but hopefully helpful. And, incidentally, I am unaccustomed to having my practices questioned."

Rachel inwardly chastised herself and was about to apologize when, without warning, something of the old Rachel Buchanan Lord came back. She stood her full height and made the stranger a victim of her dark glare.

"And I, sir, am unaccustomed to having a *gentleman* be rude to me without cause!"

To Rachel's total surprise he laughed suddenly. "The lady has spirit. The lady is also right. I owe her an apology," he said from the corner of his mouth as if addressing an audience.

His laugh was disarming. Rachel felt tears of frustration gather in her eyes and turned away in hopes that he would not see.

"Shall we start over? I am Dr. Maynard Killjoy, recently from the Portland Sanatorium and before that an internist at Boston University. And you are—?"

"I am Rachel Lord," she said with quiet dignity.

Dr. Killjoy was visibly taken aback. "You are—you mean you are Mrs. *Colby* Lord? I didn't know—you must believe that—"

"Do you only apologize to a chosen few?" she asked coldly, choking back the tears at mention of Cole's full name.

Maynard Killjoy sighed and picked up his bag. "I seem to be doing everything wrong. But, yes, it does make a difference. I will need your help if we hope to bring Miss Lee back from the conscious coma she is in—"

"Conscious coma?" Rachel was questioning him again, but she felt no obligation to behave otherwise. Yolanda was her dearest friend. And what was she to him? Still, if he could help—

"I use that lay term to explain a condition into which the patient has lapsed because she is unable to face the tragedy. She hears us but is unable to respond. That way she feels no pain and is falsely secure in a world of her own creation."

"Her suffering is too much—she may never come back—"

"You did."

Anger came to Rachel's rescue again. "That doesn't mean I suffered any less pain!"

"No—no, it doesn't mean that at all. It means that you dealt with it."

*I didn't deal with it. I may never deal with it,* Rachel's heart cried out as she turned to make an escape.

But suddenly two strong hands were on her arms, detaining her. And then it was as if she were looking into the face of another man. "Don't go." His voice was almost pleading. "Tell me everything you can—unless it hurts too much?"

The request was a question, but Rachel chose not to answer it. Instead, she told of Yolanda's bright, cheerful nature—her energy, her inability to sit still. Then, skipping several chapters, she went directly into the tragic events of Yolanda's wedding day.

"So it is easy to understand her anguish." Rachel finished, "even," she added pointedly, "for a dull-normal being like myself."

"You are quite extraordinary, Mrs. Lord," Dr. Killjoy said coolly, "but I feel that there is something else—something I must reach for. Are you sure you've left nothing out concerning Miss Lee?"

"Nothing important," Rachel said. "And now, if you will excuse me, I have some other matters that need attending. I will be at the Meeting House should you need me. And I hope you find your accommodations to your liking for the time being."

"I'm sure I will be comfortable," he said. "And I plan to remain as long as it takes to bring your friend from the other world she's in. She *will* come back, you know."

The conviction in his voice was music to Rachel's ears. No matter how arrogant the man was, all that was required of him was to help Yolanda know how much she was loved, needed, and prayed for.

Buried in her thoughts, Rachel was unaware that the two of them had descended the narrow stairs which led from the outside to the rough-floored upper deck. At the bottom she paused and said a stiffly polite thank you to Dr. Killjoy— her eyes on the Meeting House instead of meeting his.

So she did not see his eyes studying her face with something akin to sympathy mixed with perplexity. But she heard his words.

"I seldom apologize—but I am sorry about your loss—" Rachel bit her lip and hurried away. *Cole, oh, Cole!*

# 15

## Unpopular Vote

Rachel slipped quietly through the door of the Meeting House and sat down on the back seat. The men, in a heated discussion, either failed to hear her or chose to ignore her presence. They were accustomed to her attending meetings, having forgiven her for being a woman, she supposed. She wondered fleetingly what they would do if their wives suddenly took the same liberty or stormed the place—

Quickly she dismissed such thoughts and tried to listen for the topic under discussion. But it was hard to concentrate. Rachel's thoughts kept going over the events of the morning. As overbearing as she found this Dr. Killjoy, Rachel had to admit there was something about him—something she was unable to put her finger on—that was magnetic. Maybe—who was to say?—that magnetism would be the power which reached into Yolanda's heart and drew out the arrow. But Yolanda was vulnerable now. Surely Maynard Killjoy was not a man who would plunge another arrow, hurting Yolanda even more?

She dismissed the thought; but another took its place: What was it the doctor said about Yolanda's being in another world? Oh, yes, that it was of her own creation. Unconsciously Rachel sighed. Just look at the worlds she herself lived in. She was—no, she must not think of that. She was not a wife. . .and yet there was no way she could put her undying love for her husband in the past tense.

*Had been* a wife—no, never, not in a million years! She would love Cole forever and ever...

The very memory of Cole set the pulse at the base of her throat beating faster, swelling, rising to her heart and moving it up to choke her. As she had done so many times before, Rachel drew three practiced breaths—deep, deep, *deep*—and forced her breathing to return to normal.

"—very popular in Portland—bringin' in money, too— chargin' only a small admittance fee—draws men from everywheres—"

The hum of the men's voices reached Rachel's ears, then faded. It seemed important that she find an identity—find out which of her worlds were of her own creation, and to which she belonged.

*I belong to God, and that world is not of my making. . . it is my reason for living. I am His and He is mine, and it is He who will see me though this and eventually take me to be reunited with Cole. . . it HAS to be that way, else other worlds will overwhelm me.*

Other worlds? The world in which she and Cole had lived? Rachel shook her head to clear it. Who could say? But there was the world of *here and now*, where she was mother, teacher, friend, and—

Rachel stopped short in her thinking. Fear, like a living thing, reached to grip her throat. She tried to rise, hoping to escape. But her legs would not support her. "Oh, Lord," she whispered brokenly. "Oh, Lord, what would *You* do?"

A soft, still voice whispered inside her, "I will never leave thee nor forsake thee."

God's promise was as sound today as when Paul had repeated it to the Hebrews—and just as comforting. "Well, Lord, You have me cornered!" Rachel whispered back. "But You'll have to be my Helper if I'm to carry on with the dream. You're right, as always—Lordsburg is Your City!"

At peace, Rachel sat erect and dismissed all thoughts

except the business at hand. It occurred to her that the voices had risen dangerously.

"We'll need a decidin' vote, seein' as how it's a draw!" The words were Brother Davey's and the little man was all but jumping up and down in his round-eyed frustration.

Rachel's eyes scanned the room for Buck, hoping to catch his eye. That would bring him to where she sat, and he could explain what was so controversial. There was the General, his back to her, the sideview of his face showing a faint look of amusement. Whatever it was could not be too serious. Marshal Hunt sat to his right, and beyond was Burt Clemmons, wearing, of all things, a coonskin cap (while undoubtedly barefoot). Rachel's eyes misted over, remembering his loyalty to Cole and Cole's acceptance of him, never trying to change his idiosyncrasies.

Blinking back the tears, she counted off the Council members—Farnall, O'Grady, Judson Lee . . .

It was Yolanda's father who caught Rachel's glance. Immediately he was on his feet. "Gentlemen! There be a lady amongst us. Watch the language, lads, and best our City Manager here be explainin'."

Buck rose. With a smile at Rachel, he said it would be well to recap for all their sakes.

"Some of the men are discussing the possibilities of a 'Bachelor's Hall,' Rachel," Buck began. "Perhaps you remember an earlier attempt in Dr. McLoughlin's time—"

"*Attempt!*" Somebody interrupted rudely. " 'Twas a success, th' way I heerd—"

Other voices joined in, all but drowning out Buck's voice. It was plain to Rachel that the emotional charge in the room went deeper than such a trivial issue. Without Cole they were like a drove of Canadian honkers who had lost the lead goose. She understood. Only the Lord knew how she understood. And yet the division of the wagon train as they headed West together came from something of no more significance.

Rachel rose to her feet. "If I understand right," she said in a loud, clear voice, "you are in need of a deciding vote. That will be mine—and I do not vote on issues until they are clear to me!"

There was a murmur, then silence. Rachel sat down as Buck went on to explain that the hall would be patterned from the original one back when James Douglas, Governor-General of British Columbia, gave scholarly talks. Wives, mostly Indian, were excluded—

Yes, and Buck was not to forget the other Douglas—David, wasn't it?—that Scotch botanist who scared the Indians with his explosives. All that educated talk, and maybe a wee bit of ale...

What would happen if there were no dignitaries to expound on politics and worldly affairs?

Well (the men hedged a little), there might be some outside entertainment...you know...

"No, she doesn't know," Buck reminded the group.

Well, riflemen to demonstrate their skill. And maybe a few dancing women. But (hastily) mostly talk, just talk.

"And where will *your* women be?" Rachel prompted. When there was no answer, she went on, "Aha! they're excluded? All right, hand me a slip of paper. I am ready to vote. Wait—on second thought, I will cast my 'No' aloud!"

There was cheering, mixed with a few jeers. But Rachel was not to be intimidated. "You invited me to vote—remember? Why not consider a family recreation hall instead? One thing leads to another in these things, as I am sure has been pointed out before I came—"

"Cain't tell them moles nothin'! Think they kin sin a little 'n git by with it—that's what!" Brother Davey crowed.

"That doesn't happen," Buck said quietly. "Rachel's right. This can be a creeping paralysis, and before we know it somebody thinks a little crack in a commandment is all right. Well, it doesn't work that way—and we owe it to Cole's memory to keep Lordsburg as clean as its name intends!"

His voice broke on the last few words, and there was complete silence as he elbowed his way through to Rachel. Suddenly she felt inexorably tired. Even greeting General Wilkes, the Marshal, and Burt would have to wait. The day had drained her completely. When Buck reached her, she took his hand and they hurried out.

Star, Mary Cole, and Moreover ran to meet them. "Aunt Em baked cookies," the children were saying. Rachel wiped their mouths absentmindedly but managed a tired smile.

"I was proud of you today," Buck said huskily.

Once Cole had said those words, but Buck could have no way of knowing how they hurt. "I am afraid it was an unpopular vote," she said.

"It was the support I needed," was all he said.

# 16

## Wanderings of the Mind

Rachel made a point of seeking out General Wilkes the next day. The gray, once frosting only his sideburns, now threaded throughout his heavy crown of hair. How distinguished he looked in his uniform! And his manners were as flawless as his dress. How many men could bend so gracefully to kiss a lady's hand without appearing foolish? Or offer gracious compliments without sounding like the brass cymbals of flattery?

"Ah, my dear Rachel, as lovely as ever. You are such an inspiration to the other ladies."

"Hardly that," Rachel smiled. "But," and, removing her hand from his, she made a small curtsy, "I thank you, sir—you are very kind."

"Not at all. You should see the faces of some of the women elsewhere—the lines of despair." He shook his head. "It makes me almost glad my dear wife did not linger in her suffering—" General Wilkes cleared his throat and shifted the chain of thought. "Their faces—bless them—look like carved dried apples, and always they wear black bonnets."

"Black? We never wear black—except—"

Rachel stopped and the General understood. Laying a fatherly arm about her shoulders, he said gently, "I know—I know, my dear. I have loved and lost, too—all the more reason I should have been here sooner."

Rachel stayed in the circle of his arms only long enough

to regain her composure. "It is enough that you came. I need you—we all do. It's just the mention of that color reminded me that we must make arrangements—"

"For the memorial service?" He released her gently. "Would it help if I took charge—that is, with the help of the others—thereby relieving you of the details?"

Rachel swallowed the hard lump in her throat. "I would appreciate it, sir," she managed—"that is, when Yolanda is ready—and I just don't know when that will be."

"Have you encountered Dr. Killjoy?"

"I guess you could call it an encounter!"

At her tart reply, General Wilkes chuckled. "Don't let his tactics offend you. He gives the impression of being— well, different. It depends on the patient."

"*I* am not his patient." Then why had she let him ruffle her?

Rachel brought the subject back to the memorial, express- ing her appreciation, and accepting the General's kind offer. They were about to part when Rachel reached out a detain- ing hand.

Something about her gesture must have communicated her need to General Wilkes. He had replaced his fringed glove. Now he quickly removed it again and placed his bare hand over hers.

"What is it, my dear? What is troubling you?"

"The dreams I had when—when Cole was away the last time—I mean, were they real? I have always wondered if it happened that way—and Cole seemed reluctant to talk—"

"About his illegal imprisonment, I am sure you mean? And, no, your husband was not reluctant to talk, my dear. It was a part of the agreement that what transpired remain secret, else his testimony might have been of no value in the conviction of the accused."

Rachel's throat filled with dust. She swallowed and tried to mouth the name. But it would not come.

"Julius Doogan," the General supplied for her. The words, spoken softly, seemed to echo like an empty tomb.

Julius Doogan passing himself off as judge, jury, and executor...holding Brother Davey and then Cole...beating them, starving them. How good to be free of him at last...

But what was the General saying? That the man who had done all these things, defied all laws, broken Yolanda's heart, and before that betrayed the wagon train—and threatened Rachel herself—was *free*?

"There were no grounds to hold him longer," the General said with regret. "Jails were overcrowded. Laws changed with statehood—and I am afraid that some of our legislators concerned themselves more with the politics of reelection, once Salem became the capital city, than with incarcerating the guilty."

"You mean—he's here somewhere—?" Rachel's words were a hoarse whisper and her heart pounded with shame at recollection of Julius Doogan's forceful hands tearing at her garments in unsuccessful attempts to seduce her.

"I would hope not. However, it is the opinion of Dr. Killjoy that the man is deranged—'criminally insane' is the phrase he used, I think—so I want you to be most careful."

Rachel wondered later if she thanked the General. Her heart pounding with humiliation and renewed fear and anger, she had hurried away. She must check on Yolanda.

At the door, Rachel hesitated in order to compose herself. She was still shaken from the news that Julius Doogan was on the loose again. Was this man so hate-filled that he would stalk her forever? No, it had to be more. But what? Wave after wave of something akin to sickness swept her body as she stood trying to exhale the breath from her lungs. But underneath it all Rachel remembered what a part the General had played in Cole's rescue...how much she owed him. She must find a way to show her appreciation, not that anything could reward him properly. And not that he would accept—

A stirring in Yolanda's room broke into Rachel's thinking. Was someone with Yolanda? Or could she have tried to get up? All thoughts turned toward Yolanda now as Rachel threw open the door with such thrust that she all but fell inside.

Two strong arms imprisoned her immediately. In the gathering darkness it was hard for Rachel to make out the outline of the face above hers. And for a moment her heart stopped. The next moment anger had come to her rescue.

"Don't you ever knock?" The baritone voice could belong to none other than the impossible doctor.

"I—I was afraid I would disturb the patient," Rachel said weakly, wrenching herself free.

The sarcasm in his low laugh made her realize how ridiculous the words sounded. But, determined to regain her composure, she swallowed hard and forced herself to meet his gaze. So what if she burst in instead of knocking!

"I'm here to see Yolanda!"

"So am I," he reminded her, still blocking the distance between them. "I do not want her left alone a moment."

"You mean," Rachel said in surprise, "that you've been here all this time—that you haven't rested?"

She noticed the tired look in his eyes and felt some of her anger subside. "I'm sorry—I didn't realize—"

Maynard Killjoy waved away her words with an impatient gesture that swept the sensitive hands in a fan-shape and then through his heavy hair. "I don't need sympathy, Mrs. Lord. I need help. What had Miss Lee had by way of medication before I came?"

Rachel thought for a moment. "Aunt Em—Mrs. Galloway—used ammonia when—when—" Rachel swallowed hard, then went on, "and I think she steeped catnip with mint, boneset—and she usually adds sage—"

The doctor nodded. "That accounts for the sweating. But mixed with the medication I've administered? Suffice it to say that I need no assistant doctors!"

Rachel drew herself up even taller. "Dr. Killjoy, we don't intend playing doctor here. We call it 'helping thy neighbor.' And," her voice rose a little, "we are not ashamed of our ways! Maybe you could profit from learning them—"

"Whoa, whoa now! Did I really deserve that? It's only that mixing potions can be dangerous—cause hallucinating, delirium, that kind of thing—"

Immediately Rachel was remorseful. Why were they quarreling when their purpose was the same? Helping Yolanda was all that mattered. "Has she shown signs?" she asked anxiously.

"She hasn't moved. And if you would just stay with her while I—" he ran quick, nervous hands over the stubble on his face, "take care of this—and have a sample of the Galloways' cooking—"

Rachel was about to remind the outspoken doctor that he did not need her help when she recalled that she seemed to be the exception—a compliment, she supposed.

Feeling his eyes on her, Rachel glanced up to meet them. "Of course I will stay—why are you staring at me?"

"I was thinking how lovely you are."

Had he hit her over the head with his pill bag, Rachel could not have been more astonished. Feeling herself color, she turned to Yolanda. The door closed softly, leaving her with a myriad of confusing thoughts.

Buried in disquieting thoughts, at first Rachel thought she only imagined the flutter of Yolanda's eyelids. Then with a little moan the pale face turned toward her and the periwinkle eyes focused. Rachel was kneeling beside her immediately.

"Yolanda—Yolanda darling?" she whispered.

"Rachel," she whispered weakly, "he was here—"

"The doctor—yes, he has been with you and will be back." Rachel stroked the sweat-soaked forehead with a loving hand while whispering an inaudible prayer.

Yolanda was attempting to shake her head, the cloud of auburn hair fanning out against the pillow and clinging wetly to her thin neck. "Not him—don't you understand? He came to get me—says it's lonely out there—knelt right where you are—"

Rachel's heart stopped, then began to pound unmercifully. Tim! Yolanda *was* hallucinating. She must get Dr. Killjoy, but to leave Yolanda now would be cruel—maybe dangerous.

"You've been ill, Yo," she soothed. "It is so easy to imagine—"

For a fleeting moment something of the old Yolanda was back. Her voice strengthened and there was no doubt that she recognized Rachel. "I sent him away—don't tell *me* I'm imagining things." A single tear rolled down the translucent cheek. "It's you—you I'm trying to help—wanted your father's address—said he had a lawyer who'd turn you inside out—helped him—because," the whisper was back, "because—has secret—ruin you—threatened me—"

Yolanda's eyes rolled back wildly and her entire body stiffened. Then she relaxed completely and closed her eyes in resignation.

"You don't believe me—"

Suddenly some invisible hand reached out to tap Rachel's shoulder, to turn her around, to remind her of something buried far back in her mind. Listen, she must listen.

"I *do* believe you, Yolanda—" Rachel thought for one frightening second that Yolanda had drifted back into the "conscious coma" Dr. Killjoy had diagnosed. Desperately she made another try: "Yolanda—*Yo!*"

There was no movement—not even when the bloodless lips murmured, "Julius—he was here—"

The great blue eyes opened then and resumed their stare into the world she had created—the world where nobody could reach her. But Yolanda had revealed something the doctor needed to know. It would answer the question he had asked about there being more than shock involved. Rachel had not seen fit to go that deeply into her friend's private world then. But now? Admittedly, even now she did not know what to do. Would Dr. Killjoy, a stranger, think them both—*peculiar*?

It was a great relief when the doctor tapped lightly, said formally "Dr. Killjoy," and entered. Rachel ran past him, not daring to meet his all-seeing eye.

It was dark outside and the air was chill. But Rachel walked slowly, feeling the need to be alone with her jumbled thoughts. If she herself could believe in her dreams, wasn't it possible that Yolanda could see through the fog of her present stage—and she shuddered—maybe Julius had been there in the flesh.

# 17

## Greater Love Hath No Man

Exhausted, Rachel hurried through hearing the children's prayers. Through the haze of fatigue, she saw Star's eyes studying her closely. Round as full moons, dark as night, they begged what her lips did not ask. *I have put too much on the tiny shoulders,* Rachel thought disjointedly, *made her into a mother—and, yes, Buck into a father—when I should be there for them to lean on. . .*

There was so much, *so much,* that needed her attention. In contradiction, others (particularly Buck) insisted that she was already doing too much "under the circumstances." Rachel thought tiredly that they were unable to put the feelings in their hearts into words, while she herself allowed her speech to flow somewhat normally while postponing the moment of truth within her. She had faced her loss, and yet she had not faced it at all.

"Will you forgive me if I save the bedtime story until later? I am so weary," she told the little girls. "I—"

Mary Cole began to whimper, but little Star, thin shoulders squared, face unreadable, took the baby's hand.

"Mother Mine is tired, *Bambino,* so I shall tell you a story—the story Uncle Buck told us—"

Mary Cole bent backward with a scream of frustration. "Don' wan' 'tory—don' wan' Unkie Buck—need my daddy—"

"Oh, my darling, my precious darling!" Rachel bent to hold the sobbing toddler to her breast. "We all do." Choking back the tears of rage at the injustice of it all, she reached out one of her arms to encompass Star as well.

"Us go? Us fin' daddy now?" The tear-stained little face, like a dewy flower raised heavenward, was so trusting that it tore Rachel's heart out. How could she ever explain?

Star, the wonder child, did it for her. "We will go when Mother Mine has rested. She will tell us when we can climb the mountain—"

"Up to hebben?" Mary Cole had stopped weeping.

"As close as we can get, I promise—now if you come with me, I shall draw you some pictures of that beautiful city—"

Rachel knew she should follow, but she could not trust herself. The two beautiful miracle children whom God had entrusted to her deserved a serene mother—one who was strong, able to take command now that the person whom they loved more than life was gone.

She fell across the bed and dropped into a heavy sleep. When she awoke the sun was streaming through the east window, warming her shoulders with its bright shawl, blinding her. Or was it a reluctance to emerge from the dream of which only faint images remained? No! She must not go back. Although she could not remember the dream, Rachel had the strange feeling that she had awakened just in time...

Even after she had prepared porridge for the children and coffee for herself, the dream haunted her. Star took Mary Cole out to play while Rachel quickly set the quarters in order for the day. And still the dream. Although something horrible would have happened, even now that she was safe, the dream emerged and receded—beckoning, yet threatening to draw her back into that black abyss.

She was relieved when Buck's familiar knock came. *One, two, three*—stop. She smiled at their signal, feeling safe just knowing that he was at the door.

Pulling the coffeepot to a hotter spot on top of the wood

range, Rachel wiped her hands on her apron, but then on second thought took it off and tossed it on the sideboard. "Coming!" she called and welcomed him inside.

"You look a little more rested," he said after a quick glance at her face. "But I have the feeling something is bothering you—anything you care to talk about?"

Rachel was about to tell him she had had a terrible shock. And then she checked herself. After all, could she expect him to put much stock in anything Yolanda might say? The very fact that she had spoken at all was still something she was wrestling with her conscience over. She had not told the doctor, so should she tell Buck? Anyhow, now that she had been forewarned, she could take care of herself. But her hand was shaking as she poured coffee in the two cups Buck had taken from the cupboard shelf.

Buck saw. "What is it, Rachel? Surely you can tell *me*—"

"Nothing," she denied, realizing then that Buck would recognize the mistruth by the tremor in her voice. Always there had been such openness between them.

"All right," she smiled in resignation. "It's a dream I had—about—I don't know what it was about, actually. Something horrible was going to happen. Somebody—" Rachel winced as a fragment of the dream came back, "I think it was Yolanda—only I don't know what happened. Oh, Buck, maybe what she said was true—"

Buck rose from his chair and circled the table to stand behind her. Gripping her shoulders tightly, he demanded to know what was going on. Then, having given herself away, Rachel was forced, under his insistent questions, to share the entire story. Brushing quickly over the doctor's attitude, she told of Yolanda's regaining complete consciousness and insisting that Julius Doogan had managed to come to her bedroom, beg her to come with him, threaten her—

"With what?" Buck ground out the words.

"I don't know—revealing how he allured her away from

her family, pretending to love her, only to dump her—he did not harm her, if one can call her unharmed with a broken spirit, but who would believe that?"

"What are you holding back, Rachel?"

It was only then that Rachel realized the full impact of Julius Doogan's demands. "Why would he want my father's address? Buck, you *do* believe this?"

"I would be inclined to dismiss it in part except that we both know Doogan's free. The General told me what he shared with you. I have a strong feeling he's up to some kind of blackmail—"

"Blackmail? But what—why—?" Rachel gasped. "Oh, it's like the bad dream I had. I wish I could remember—"

But Buck was not listening. He pulled her to her feet and drew her to him, his touch as tender as if he were handling a fragile piece of china. "You must be careful—very careful— if anything happened to you, I couldn't bear it, my darling."

Rachel stood on tiptoe and brushed his cheek with a kiss, loving the smell of shaving soap and bay rum mixed with something she could only call a "masculine scent" of clean flesh that belonged exclusively to Buck. "I feel the same way about you—I couldn't bear Cole's death without you."

She did not see the look of sadness that crossed his clean-shaven face. She only heard his soothing voice: "Cole is a man we both loved deeply. Our common grief."

There was a moment's silence, and then Buck asked if she felt like talking about the memorial service. Rachel explained that General Wilkes had asked if he could take charge, to which Buck nodded. "He loves you very much, you know."

"Just as I love him," Rachel said absently. "Buck, we might as well go ahead with the service. Yolanda will be unable to go—and perhaps it is best—"

"I will talk with the General—and when this is over, there are matters you and I must discuss. Meantime, I will stay very near—"

"Good!" Rachel replied, feeling tears mist her eyes as he turned to go.

At the door he stopped. "We must contact the attorney. Or, have you by chance had a letter from him? His name is James Haute."

Letter? No, she had received no letter—or had she? Rachel remembered for the first time the fat envelope she had laid aside when, at the height of her grief, Willie Mead had delivered it along with the telegram from General Wilkes. What had become of it?

"A letter came," she said vaguely, wondering why she felt uneasy. "I'll look around for it. This lawyer—do you know him?"

"Only of him. Cole chose him because of their continued association in dividing mine shares." Buck paused, then shifted the train of thought as if to get away from further mention of the mine. "James Haute follows a strict code of ethics, according to his reputation—a letter-of-the-law attorney."

Rachel nodded, but her thoughts were elsewhere. A lawyer, Yolanda had said. Julius Doogan had a lawyer. But it was foolish to make any connection. Better to concentrate on the letter.

Buck seemed reluctant to leave her, and Rachel was equally reluctant to have him go. Buck was so warm, so comforting—like a pair of high-quality shoes worn just long enough that they knew every bone and nerve ending of their owner. Well, what a dull analogy! Buck certainly deserved better than that.

She was unaware that she smiled until Buck said, "I praise our Maker for whatever brought on that smile—oh, Rachel—"

Then, with a jerk, he opened the door, stepped out, and slammed it behind him. Was he angry? But why? What had she done? Rachel came near to running after him. And perhaps, she was to think later, their lives would have been far different if she had. . .

● ● ●

Rachel was relieved when Aunt Em came to tell her that the memorial service was set for sundown Friday—" 'Iffen it meets with your pleasure,' bein' how th' General put it. Now, Dearie, y'll let me help, there bein' something y'need?"

Rachel hugged the capable woman who had become a mother to her, then waved her away. She needed to be alone with her thoughts. Too, she must look for the letter—and, of course, consult the doctor on whether to try and get through to Yolanda on what was happening. Of course, she knew better than he that Yolanda was capable of hearing once the invisible wall was cracked. She sighed at the thought of trying to explain anything to that young man.

It would be a relief, she thought, when all this was over, when she could bury herself in day-to-day living. God intended man to work. Well, her work was cut out.

Try as she would, Rachel was unable to find the elusive letter. It seemed to have disappeared into thin air. But she did manage a time alone with Yolanda. Advised in quiet tones at the door of plans to go ahead with the memorial service, Dr. Killjoy was surprisingly receptive.

"It would be a foolhardy thing to try to transport the patient. I am glad you recognize that."

Rachel held back a sharp retort. "You will tell her?"

A look of something akin to scorn crossed the handsome face. "*Tell* her?" The tone was low and furious. Then, for no apparent reason, his voice softened. "I am tired—bone tired—"

Rachel hardened her heart against any compassion but did offer to stay with Yolanda while he had coffee and freshened up. It was mostly, she admitted to herself, to be alone with Yolanda.

When she was sure he was out of hearing distance, Rachel told Yolanda in simple terms how the men they loved were to be honored. But the wide blue eyes were unseeing, and there was no sign that Yolanda understood.

Rachel took the thin, blue-veined hand wearing the simple wedding band in her own, stroking it gently. And the tears she shed were not for herself and Cole as much as for Yolanda and Tim. A wedding was all she had—just a ceremony, not a marriage at all—while Rachel had memories of a love that was stronger than death.

•  •  •

On Friday the skies were sullen. Rachel, refusing to wear black, looked through her small closet for something neutral but a little less depressing. The gray dress? Yes, without the pink ruffling it would do fine. A black veil to show—*oh, dear God, have mercy*—widowhood...

Rachel never clearly remembered having Buck help her into the buckboard wagon, being jostled along the rut-grooved road, or Buck's holding her hand as she struggled with the wide skirt while trying to step down to the ground. What she did remember was the leveled-off top of Superstition Mountain as she raised her eyes to view for the first time what was now her husband's grave.

Thoughtfully, the men had cleared away the rubble. Only solidified lava, like frozen waterfalls, remained as a reminder of the inferno that had taken place just a month ago.

Then, as if the sun had been watching the clock, it burst forth from the gray clouds to reach searchlights up and down the mountainsides—pausing longer at the shining seams in the mountain's ribs, then moving on, only to return in wider beams. And then, in a burst of glory, the entire mountain was gilded in gold. And at the mountain's feet was the eternal river, rising and falling like a giant beast breathing in and out the very breath of life.

It was "the shining mountain above the great river" of Indian lore that Cole had shared with her. Here was a revelation—brilliant and dazzling, illuminating but not revealing its secrets of unparalleled riches, its hidden wisdom of the universe. *Superstition Mountain was to be allowed to return to its place in God's nature of things—a hallowed ground, and not an idol that gold had made of it.*

Rachel came back to the present when she realized that Buck was studying her sunlit face. "It's almost like you underwent a transfiguration."

"No more mining," she whispered. "The mountain belongs to those who rest there—the Indians, the Chinese . . . Tim . . . Cole . . ." Rachel's voice wavered and stopped.

Buck, holding back tears, guided her unfeeling feet to her rightful place behind the long, solemn procession. The trip up the narrow path was familiar, and yet it was as if she had never traveled it before—as if—*as if Star were right and they were going as close to heaven as God allowed.*

The sun receded behind gray curtains, taking with it the sheen it had brought to the mountain they were ascending in silence. But the revelation remained as Rachel stumbled when her pointed, high-topped shoes hit the slippery soil and felt Buck's steadying arm. It was all the way Cole would have wished, Rachel thought, raising her head proudly. The General led the way, attired in full-dress cavalry blues, his hat brim pulled slightly lower then regulation, wearing gold epaulets instead of the customary straps across the shoulders of his three-quarter-length coat, and his sword by his side. Rachel thought her heart would break when she saw that he was leading "Hannibal," the riderless black stallion . . . the symbol of a fallen comrade.

Trying to regain her composure, she saw that Brother
Davey, open Bible in hand, followed closely behind the
General, then Marshal Hunt and Burt Clemmons (both in
uniform, so they had served with the General?)...the
Council...and Aunt Em directly ahead of her and Buck—
carrying Mary Cole and leading Star...Yolanda's family,
the ten brothers so white-faced that their freckles stood out
comically. Rachel smiled tenderly. *God bless them—God
bless them all.*

At the top, the procession stopped and Rachel was ushered
ahead. Fleetingly she heard the faint strains of faraway
music...Mr. Solomon's violin, playing atop some unfinished building as he had played on Yolanda's wedding
day. Sad...sweet...haunting...memory-filled.

"O death, where is thy vict'ry?" Brother Davey's voice
intoned. It was balm for Rachel's bleeding heart and comfort
for all true believers. But would it be enough to sustain her
in the lonely days ahead? Instinctively her hand clutched
Buck's a little tighter.

Her mind wandered a bit then—going back in memories,
the pleasant and unpleasant, atop Superstition Mountain.
Her first trip with Yolanda...meeting Cole here, then Julius
Doogan's sudden appearance...her chance meeting with
Cole and sharing his mackinaw in a rain squall...the mining...even the strange superstitions beginning with Indian
legends, then embellished by the story-loving Scotch-Irish.
Why, she wondered, had Agnes Grant refused to come
today, choosing (she claimed) to "watch over things—what
with all th' trouble still tailin' us." Nobody paid much
attention to the tongue-wagging woman. But Rachel remembered with a shudder seeing her perched on a tall chair,
watching the settlers leave—her beady eyes much like those
of a vulture.

Rachel had missed some of the ceremony. Maybe she did
not want to hear...could not bear it. She had thought of

everything except the final incident—the one that was too much to bear.

It was with surprise that she felt Buck gently uncurling her fingers from around his hands, heard him ask if she was all right, then saw him move up to close the service.

Cole had followed a dream, Buck said. That dream had brought him West to convert a small corner of the wilderness into a Promised Land...Cole, the trusted leader, had gone on ahead...leaving the others to follow his dream... make the city he envisioned as near the Lord's "ideal" as possible...then await their calling or the return of the Lord, who would create a new heaven and earth where peace and justice would reign...remembering that "greater love hath no man than this, that a man lay down his life for his friends."

Buck closed with the passage from John, then came to hand a single red rose to Rachel. As if in a dream, she walked as near the gaping mouth of the cave-in as was safe and, with Buck's hand supporting her elbow, leaned over and dropped the blossom into the cavern. As she did so, she was almost sure she saw the painted bodies of Indians slipping close—then closer. She all but cried out, then realized that perhaps they were here out of curiosity. If not, it was best to remain calm.

Anyway, it was hard to see. Twilight was settling over the woods, collecting shadows, blending them into what would be total darkness in a few minutes—a time when the red man did not venture out. Or—*horrors!*—could there have been a raid?

She was about to whisper her fears to Buck when a piercing scream split the air and a figure in white darted past. *Yolanda!*

# 18

❧❧❧

# Out of the Depths,
# O Lord!

Rachel was never sure what happened. Her first impulse was to run to Yolanda's rescue, to hold her back from what she was sure was certain death. What was it that Yolanda had said about Tim's needing her—or was it Julius, who somehow slithered past the doctor as he may have dozed for an instant? Something about his being lonely.

"I must help her—" Rachel remembered trying to explain to Buck, who was lifting her up and seating her on Hannibal while the General spoke to her in soothing tones. One or the other mounted the black stallion to ride behind her. But this was not right either...only she and Cole rode together like this. She tried to explain, but her throat constricted.

Yolanda's voice had cut through the air, lancing the silence of the horrified mourners. "I *want* to go...I can't go on...Tim loved me...was the only man who loved me. *Let me go...we can be together in the afterworld...*"

*She must have come dangerously near the rim of the bottomless pit because there were screams of horror, all in unison like a choir. And then above the din of whispered sighs spelling relief, Rachel vaguely heard the voice of Maynard Killjoy. But that was not right either. Yolanda was wearing her wedding gown...who did he think he was, the groom?*

All the way down the mountain, Rachel, forgetting

Yolanda, was sure she saw painted bodies...riding wild-eyed ponies...darting in and out among the shadows—splicing them together with their fiery arrows...splitting the night with their bloodcurdling screams. Why did the silent procession move on as stiffly erect as cardboard cutouts, their faces expressionless?

At the base of the mountain, the others climbed into their wagons without conversation. But Rachel, one man behind her and the other leading the stallion, did not make the change. She was conscious only of the bobbing lanterns that cut through the dark like falling stars and the squeak of harness as the wagons moved forward. Then she concentrated on the pool of light cast by the lantern held by the man leading Hannibal. In its glow she watched the horse's hooves cut crescents in the sweeping mass of tall grasses, crushing the life from wild violets. But she knew that the blue-eyed flowers would spring up behind her—just as she must rise up.

Nature restores itself. Someday the mountain would be beautiful again. And below it—here she must start anew.

Buck refused to leave her, and Rachel was too drained to protest. She allowed herself to be helped into bed and covered with Nola Lee's gift, the Double Wedding Ring quilt...one ring for her...one for Yolanda...

"Out of the depths, O Lord, hear my cry..." her stiff lips tried to say.

Buck understood. Wonderful Buck...wonderful friend... who could fix everything except her heart. His light kiss told her so.

*Why, Lord, WHY?* Rachel's heart cried out as she drifted to the edge of blessed darkness. *What has happened that we are unable to celebrate a marriage—or bury our dead—without another catastrophe? Out of the depths, O Lord...*

● ● ●

In the days that followed—four of them, unless Rachel lost count—Buck and Aunt Em once again hovered over her. She obediently drank the broth, which she hated, and even drank a bit of Aunt Em's concoction of horseradish and mustard seed (and goodness knew what else) in order to stall off a house call from Dr. Killjoy. Her emotional refusal caused Buck and Aunt Em to exchange puzzled glances, which Rachel pretended not to see.

But Aunt Em was bent on giving her a report of the impression that Dr. Killjoy's dedication to his patient had made on the villagers. "Why, he hasn't left th' child's bedside for a minute since th'—since she came down with the setback, poor darlin'. He'd have fasted iffen I hadn't took him some solid vittles. Folks is hopin' he's gonna stay— an', Dearie, you'n the Council oughta give it some thought, when you're well enough t'think."

When Rachel made no reply, Aunt Em straightened the bedcovers, tucking them beneath the featherbed neatly at the corners. But there was a question in her face as she left.

Rachel watched from the window, making sure Aunt Em had forgotten nothing that would bring her back. Then she put an experimental foot on the floor, feeling for her slippers. Ignoring the dizziness that threatened to sweep her from her feet, she cautiously tried her legs. When she was sure they would support her, she pulled a long black skirt from the closet. The first blouse her fingers touched would do. Yes, the white muslin with muttonleg sleeves was fine. At first she considered removing the black ribbon lacing the neck. But why bother? She was only going to see Yolanda and that impossible doctor. He would try to turn her back, of course. Well, let him try!

At Yolanda's door Rachel paused to wipe the beads of perspiration from her forehead. She was surprised at how weak she was. Her stomach growled, reminding her that she had left Aunt Em's tray of coddled eggs and sourdough biscuits untouched. She pressed her middle with her fist and felt no surprise that it felt shrunken. All she could hope was that another such rumble would not divulge her condition to Maynard Killjoy. No way was she going to submit to an examination from him!

In the brief pause, Rachel realized that Yolanda's voice was going nonstop. At first she was unable to make out the words either because of their incoherence or because of the ringing in her own ears.

Then the words became more clear. Yolanda was baring her soul!

". . . not that I resented her happiness. I love her too much for that. But," and there was a pitiful little sob, so uncharacteristic of the vibrant Yolanda, "you see—you understand I wanted men to love me—love me the way they love Rachel—"

At the sound of her name, Rachel almost fell against the door. Yolanda—why, Yolanda was surely not jealous of her—

And then Yolanda was speaking again. "We used to dream—make up lists, you know, about the men we hoped to marry—oh, this must sound foolish—"

The doctor's voice was low and compelling. "It does not sound foolish at all," he said gently. "I want to hear more."

"Well, I *do* remember respect—only then it was not at the top of our list . . . we thought of physical appearances and—and wanting to be loved. That's why I went away with Julius—"

"Julius?"

And then Yolanda told of her shame. "Only—only—" she floundered for words, "I don't want you to think—the worst. I am still—" Yolanda paused and then spoke with some of the old spirit, "I remain the foolish virgin!"

"That is nothing to be ashamed of—or apologetic for."

Rachel heard the sob that caught in Yolanda's throat. "No," she said tiredly now, "but when I met Tim I thought it would be enough . . . having him love *me* . . . now I don't know—except that I am left with nothing . . . *nothing* . . . NOTHING!"

Rachel was about to tiptoe away when she heard mention of her name again, this time by Dr. Killjoy.

"Rachel has nothing—if you choose to put it that way—either, Miss Lee—"

"Yolanda." The single-word correction was muffled—spoken, Rachel felt sure, from the circle of the doctor's arms. All in the line of his profession? Either way, she must not be discovered. She should leave but felt rooted to the spot.

"Yolanda—yes, that is better. Your friend has not fooled me with her bravado. It is the facade to hide a broken heart. I have offended her, but it is too early to apologize for trying to help with a shock system of my own."

Rachel hardly knew whether to be angry or relieved. Either way, she was not going to change her assessment of him until he proved himself. And then she wondered why it mattered.

She was about to make a successful getaway when her stomach growled even louder. In an effort to silence the rumble, she grasped at the doorknob and all but fell inside.

The laughter which greeted her was the last thing she expected. To be accused of eavesdropping would be understandable—even in order. To be scolded for interrupting, likewise. But laughing? Had the whole world gone berserk? Because without warning she found herself laughing too.

Yolanda, her dearest friend, had reached bottom and was climbing out. *So the Lord heard my cry,* Rachel marveled.

# 19

## To Follow the Dream

June tiptoed in softly. Tiny buds of springtime burst and almost overnight made the valley into a leafy bower. Aunt Em's rose garden seemed determined to outdo the mountainsides of wild larkspur—each spicing the air with its own fragrance. But Rachel was too busy to notice.

There were still missing pieces of the strange events which had blighted her life and Yolanda's forever. Some of them perhaps she would find as time moved on . . . others she might never know. And the truth was that it was best, in her mind, not to dig too deeply. Unbearable pain lay just below the surface of the day-by-day pattern she was trying to establish. A few details remained, and then she must devote her full life to the pursuit of Cole's dream.

Yolanda, after being mired in despondency so long and finally in desperation taking the near-fatal step of ending her life, changed dramatically. "She's not the same Yolanda," Rachel said to Buck, "but—" and her voice dropped to a thin whisper, "I'm not either."

Buck reached out a hand as if to touch her and then drew it back, seeming warned by something in her eyes. "None of us are, Rachel—don't you know that? Nothing is the same, but life moves forward and we must move with it—"

She nodded quickly. "Yes, and we must move Cole's dream ahead. Otherwise we have lost him."

A little muscle twitched in Buck's jaw, and then he spoke

matter-of-factly. "Lordsburg? The attorney will be here next week. As soon as the provisions are clear to us, we'll go ahead. Same Council? Same everything?"

"I'll stand by until it's done—but, Rachel, there are other things we need to discuss—"

"Yes, there are, but nothing we can't postpone."

Rachel was looking toward the Meeting House and did not see the searching look in his eyes, which had turned to near-mahogany as they studied her or the look of hurt at what he found in her face. She was concentrating on the date. School should be out by now . . . perhaps a picnic and the formality of handing out report cards. "Then next year a new Amity School . . . a new church . . ." she said, completely out of context.

Mention of the picnic brought a look of panic to Yolanda's face. "Do we dare?" Her white face frightened Rachel. "I mean—every time we try to—to—oh, Rachel, it hurts!"

"I know, darling, but, as Buck says, we have to go on." She paused, then said with concern, "are you up to it?"

"Preparing for the end of school? I don't know—maybe I am—yes, yes, I am. But the other? No."

"What other, Yo?"

"Another love—love of any kind. I am no longer capable of loving—another man—or—" Yolanda paused, then seemed to rephrase her thoughts. "Oh, I guess I believe in God, but something is gone—let's call it my faith in His caring."

"Yolanda, don't!" Rachel cried out.

She had been about to say more when General Wilkes joined them. After his cordial greeting, he asked Rachel's permission to visit with her the following evening. She smiled at his formality. Since when had he deemed it necessary to ask permission?

With a slight bow, the General was about to walk

away when he turned to ask, "Has either of you two lovely ladies seen Mrs. Grant since—well, for some time now?"

Rachel thought back to the fateful night of the pilgrimage up Superstition Mountain—and seeing Agnes Grant's beady eyes following every move. But before she could speak, Yolanda was saying something which shocked Rachel into silence.

"She—that woman—Mrs. Grant stayed behind that night—remember? And Indians came. They surrounded the village, closing in on her—her and some other man. I don't know who he was."

"Thank you, Mrs. Norval. I shall look into it."

With his usual military stride, the General walked away.

Yolanda spoke first. "Don't tell me I'm crazy. I—I saw them, I *did*!"

"If you have taken leave of your senses, so have I!" Rachel retorted. "Only I hesitated to repeat what I saw—"

Yolanda exhaled. "And I was afraid to tell Maynard—Dr. Killjoy—"

They exchanged versions and decided that the Indians had taken advantage of the settlers' absence and come for the skull that Agnes Grant had in her possession. Maybe the woman was frightened away. Or could the Indians have taken her? What a horrible fate—

"But General Wilkes has offered to check on her—Yolanda, who was with her? I have a feeling you recognized him."

"I don't know," Yolanda said. But her eyes were cast downward, and the way she fingered with her cotton skirt said otherwise.

"Was it—could it have been—?"

But before Rachel could say Julius Doogan's name, Yolanda interrupted her. "He's in love with you, you know."

"*Who?*"

"Why, the General, of course."

"You *are* out of your mind!" Rachel gasped.

• • •

The next day Yolanda moved home. Dr. Killjoy would not listen to her arguments that she would be safe alone, that she had grown up here and knew how to take care of herself. Over her protests, he had the stable boy bring his long-axle, deep-carmine buggy to the hotel entrance. Curiously, some of the men who had been sitting on the edge of the gallery stopped their whittling and gathered around to examine the rig and the sorrel mare harnessed between the polished oak shafts. Several whistled in awe. Then, self-consciously, they returned to their whittling when they saw the doctor escorting his patient out the door—still watching from beneath their hat brims.

Rachel was watching from her own window, and when Dr. Killjoy and Yolanda appeared she hurried down. Yolanda, she noticed, looked very fit. Her once-shrunken cheeks had plumped to their usual roundness, and her hair, always lovely, was even more so in the June-morning sunlight. The indigo cotton dress made her blue eyes rivals for the fields of larkspur along the foothills. But there was something else—a sort of shine—as Maynard Killjoy carefully helped her onto the step and into the buggy. The doctor had left the top off, and when Yolanda started to put on her bonnet, he put out a restraining hand.

"Leave it off," he said with obvious admiration in his voice. Then, seeing Rachel's eyes on the two of them, he looked a little flustered. "The sun's good for you!"

The three exchanged greetings, and Yolanda asked if Friday would be all right for the end-of-school picnic.

The doctor answered for her. "We shall see," he said

curtly, with something akin to combat in his voice.

*We?* Rachel held back a sharp retort. Yolanda obviously did not mind his bossy manner in the least. Rachel returned to her quarters feeling confused and, as usual, irritated by the doctor's arrogance.

To Rachel's surprise, however, Dr. Killjoy put his stamp of approval on the plans. He dropped by briefly later in the day to deliver a note from Yolanda. She thanked him stiffly and then regretted bothering when she saw that, although he did not smile, his lips trembled with the need to. For some reason this exasperating man enjoyed goading her— then found her displeasure amusing.

Well, two could play the game. Letting her lips curve slowly upward into a little smile, Rachel gave him a look of wide-eyed innocence. *How's that for a smoke screen, Doctor?*

"Would you like to come in for coffee?" she asked sweetly.

His amusement died quickly. Caught off-guard, Dr. Killjoy's authoritative manner changed to speculation and then to schoolboy shyness.

"I—I have an appointment," he hedged, his voice low and a little awkward. And for a fleeting moment a strange light illuminated his eyes, sending her a private message which she was to spend the day trying to decode. "Another time, perhaps?"

"Perhaps," Rachel murmured, wondering who won the game.

But she must concentrate on tonight...then on Friday ...then on next week, when the lawyer would arrive. Then on following her husband's dream.

# 20

## Bewildering Proposal

For reasons she would have been unable to explain, Rachel dressed with unusual care that evening in preparation for General Wilkes' call. Choosing a simple but elegant and gauze-thin batiste of willow-green, she added a strand of pearls. Examining her carefully braided hair in the mirror, she saw that wisps were already escaping to curl about her forehead, around her ears, and down the nape of her neck. Just the way Cole liked it, Rachel remembered—*oh, Darling!*

When the General appeared at her door, Rachel thought he looked a little distracted. But his compliment was gracious.

"Ah, my dear Rachel, you look ravishing," he said with his usual little formal bow.

Rachel thanked him, and as they made small talk she examined his face with genuine affection. Such a nice face! A face that revealed the character of the fine man who had meant so much in Cole's work here. The man who then rescued him. A face one could trust, depend on . . . compassionate, imaginative . . . grooved with lines of suffering but unembittered . . .

Rachel realized suddenly that the General had stopped talking and was looking at her quizzically. She felt her cheeks color, and in an effort to hide her embarrassment she blurted out a barrage of questions. General Wilkes did not seem to notice that she was flustered.

Yes, he had found Agnes Grant. And, obviously unaware of Rachel and Yolanda's knowledge, he told of the appearance of the Indians. What tribe? He did not know, but any spark could ignite a fire, there being so much unrest on the reservations, complaints of the "Bostons" having robbed them of their land and its livelihood as well as their horses, squaws, and dogs—all of which the red man counted his wealth.

"Their *wives*? But we would never do that—"

"No, my dear, *we* would not. But, in the sad state of human affairs, there do exist men who would, even though idealists like your late husband and I have *remained* idealists."

"What brought them here—and what took them away?" Rachel gasped. "The Indians, I mean."

The General inhaled in a way that was almost a sigh. Rachel noticed how tired his voice sounded in reply. "There is a distinct possibility that the question is not *what* but *who*? The woman had an Indian skull in her possession—have you the stomach for this, my dear?"

At her nod, he continued. "I found some other Indian artifacts as well—items which I confiscated for our protection. The Indians took the skull for burial. That is why they appeared as we returned from the memorial service. Now as to *who*, it is best not to speculate. Suffice it to say that there is a white agitator behind this—one with ulterior motives. Therefore, although I do not wish to alarm you unnecessarily, I am compelled to beg that you be cautious. You see, you may be—shall I say a target?"

"*I?*" The single word was a dry whisper.

"There, there, I *have* upset you, and I came here to offer my protection. Let us speak of other matters—"

The pale eyes of Julius Doogan swam in front of her as Rachel excused herself to put the children to bed. Of course he would come back. And yet what for? It made no sense.

Sunk in her thoughts, Rachel did not hear the General's

knock on the door leading to the small bedroom. It was Star who opened the door and said, "Please to come in, Senor."

Mary Cole clung to Rachel's skirt. "Go 'way—go 'way!"

"It's all right, Darling," Rachel soothed, picking the baby up and then speaking to General Wilkes, "I hope you understand—"

"Indeed I do! Loss is a terrible thing for a child." Then, turning to Mary Cole, he said, "I know a story—"

Mary Cole bent backward in a near-tantrum. "Don' wan' 'tory—want Daddy—*need* Daddy—you not my daddy!"

"Some other time then," he offered with a note of sadness. "No, dear child, I am not your father. No man will ever be that. But I have an idea—perhaps you would like a grandfather?"

" 'ave Gran'pa Davey—go 'way!"

It was Star's matchless wisdom that quieted the child.

"It is all right that we should have two grandfathers, *Bambino*," she said in silvery tones. "God gave us two in the beginning."

Mary Cole's great eyes—so like Cole's—searched the General's face. She made no reply, but she stopped crying.

The General stood at attention as Rachel knelt to hear the children's prayers. Although he did not kneel with them, he added a soft "Amen" at the close.

Back in the living room, Rachel poured coffee and set out a plate of molasses cookies she had baked. "I remembered your fondness for these," she smiled as the General seated her.

She had intended to apologize further for Mary Cole's behavior, but it was plain to see that General Wilkes had something on his mind. So she was silent as she offered sugar and cream. It was the General who broke the silence.

"Are you going ahead with plans for building the house— the one you and Cole had planned?"

Rachel had been unable to visit the rough scaffolding

which outlined what would have been a near-mansion. Someday she must, of course. The decision could wait until then. But now her heart was too freshly scarred. "I don't know," was all she could manage.

"We could do it together," he said softly. "I know it is too soon—but there are reasons why I must speak what is in my heart—Rachel, will you marry me?"

At first Rachel was sure she misunderstood. No, she had heard distinctly. But she was too bewildered to answer.

Noting her astonishment, General Wilkes laid a fatherly hand over Rachel's left hand. Then, picking the hand up, he gently stroked each finger, pausing on the fourth to look pensively at the flashing diamond which had brought such joy and such sorrow.

"I know I could never make up for your loss—or take Cole's place—"

"Nobody could," Rachel said rigidly. "I will never love again...that is, be *in* love...*never.*"

The General sighed and continued to look deeply into the brilliant stone as if remembering a love of his own. "Time is a healer," he said, as if talking to himself. "Memories fade, leaving gentle paths in the heart. But the loneliness remains. I live by the verse in Hebrews which seems to speak to me: 'He taketh away the first that he may establish the second.' Yes, my dear Rachel, you will love again—"

When Rachel would have protested, General Wilkes returned her hand to her lap and placed a silencing finger to her lips. "Just hear me out—" He leaned back and squared his already erect shoulders. Then, as if he had garnered courage—or was it strength?—he continued. "Unfortunately, I will not be that man. I am 30 years your senior—and—there are risks in my work—also I—"

"General Wilkes!" Rachel was alarmed by something in his voice. She could not bear another loss. Not now.

"Don't be alarmed, my dear. Death has become...if not

a friend, not exactly an enemy. Shall I say a companion? I perhaps do not speak often enough of my faith, but I am at peace with the Lord—"

"Oh, sir, I am sure you are!" Rachel exclaimed with a surge of affection. "It's just that you find death so easy to talk about while I—"

"Your grief is new, and you must pass through the dark tunnel of despair, rebellion, and depression. And," he brought the subject back to his proposal, "I would be there—the shoulder you need to lean on. Not," he smiled, "as a lover or even a husband in the usual sense of the word—let's say the father. I never had a daughter, you know. I would draw up the proper papers when James Haute arrives—"

Rachel looked at him in question, "You mean—?"

"Cole's attorney is also mine. He knows of my wealth. You see, I have built up a small fortune over the years—and, sadly, there is nobody to whom I can leave it."

"Money has nothing to do with it." Rachel paused, wondering how to explain. "And it isn't even a matter of love. I love you dearly, General Wilkes, and your talk of—of leaving makes me sad. But, you see, I have plenty of money—"

"For yourself and perhaps for your children. But the city? Let me help you build it! It would be a joy, a privilege, I assure you. My proposal is purely selfish—not one of self-sacrifice at all. And I would be kind to you, protect you—"

A tear, rebellious at being too long withheld, slid down Rachel's hot cheek and she felt a breeze come through the open window to kick at her curls. "I can't," she whispered brokenly.

The General stood and drew Rachel to her feet. "We do not make sudden decisions here on the frontier. I beg you to think on it."

# 21

## Warning of Danger!

Rachel did think on the matter. All night, as the June breeze played in the trumpet vines outside the bedroom window, her troubled mind kept reviewing the strange proposal. In a way it would be another marriage of convenience—only one with a less exciting ending. No, she thought as she tossed restlessly, her marriage to Cole—solely for the purpose of getting away from her drunken father's threats—did not end happily after all. If only time could have stood still on the memorable night when the little inn leaning against the hill opened its welcoming arms to them, begging them to consummate their love...or, when they were reunited following Cole's captivity...

At that thought Rachel sat straight up in bed, a sudden realization washing her entire being. It was as if a voice spoke out of the darkness: *He saved your husband—brought him back to you. But for him Cole would have lost his life. Are you not in his debt?*

But the General would not wish her to accept his proposal out of gratitude. Marriage for any reason other than love was a sacrilege. And then her tortured thoughts went back to her wrong reason for marrying Cole. But the pain of remembering how their love had grown into a union of shining splendor hurt too much.

Returning to thoughts of the General's kind offer, Rachel considered the mutual convenience of the terms. No demands, he had said. He would just care for her and protect her, nothing more. And for himself he asked so small a token—only an end to his loneliness while together they prepared a legacy: the fulfillment of Cole's dream. It was so little to ask—just the opportunity to protect her. Protect her from what or whom?

A marriage of mutual convenience? That would mean saying farewell to love—the kind of love that came once in a lifetime. Or had she done that already? Here was a man who offered her unswerving kindness. And certainly there would be respect and respectability. They would be friends. Certainly, most widows here in the settlement would find such an offer rewarding. But she was not like "most widows" any more than her marriage to Cole was like "most marriages." They had something sacred—so special that it could not be duplicated. She must say no.

Rachel dozed fitfully and awoke in a state of exhaustion. On impulse she decided to get the children fed and dressed and to take a stroll out of the village. She needed to think— alone. Then, hopefully refreshed, she would return and prepare for the picnic. Aunt Em would be happy to keep an eye on Star and Mary Cole.

Something seemed to guide her feet. Hardly aware that she crossed the Village Green, Rachel found herself heading in the general direction of the acreage that Cole had set aside for their home. At first she walked slowly. Then, as if drawn by some invisible magnet, her feet set a hurried pace. Rachel's heartbeat responded, and she felt suddenly invigorated. It seemed important that she visit the spot.

At the site she stopped, overwhelmed by an unexplainable depression. What had she hoped for, anyway? To see Cole's head bent down studying the blueprints, one unruly lock of hair falling boyishly forward to offset the lines of concentration in his face? Rachel winced, knowing she should not have come. And yet she seemed unable to leave.

Standing there, almost against her will, Rachel suddenly saw the house clearly in its finished state. Its bare ribs would flesh out with heavy clapboard siding to cover the great two-story house. Inside there would be dark paneling—room after room of it. A library lined with leatherbound books. A drawing room, parlor, kitchen, pantry, servants' quarters . . . furnished in excellent taste . . . but dark . . . a feel of gloom and weight prevailing. Rachel jerked erect. She was thinking—why she was thinking in terms of what General Wilkes might choose! A house needed sunlight to be a home—sunlight and a feeling of airiness. It should be filled with the smell of rising bread and the laughter of many children . . .

The dark vision faded and, without conscious bidding on Rachel's part, another appeared: a grove of trees, and in the center a small cottage—or was it a log cabin?—with wide-open windows to inhale the sweetness of an orchard in spring and to exhale the spice of gingerbread. Flowers and more flowers, daffodils in never-ending lines, tulips clumping along the picket fence rows like Dutch children in their wooden shoes . . . forsythia . . . flowering quince . . . and a little rustic bridge crossing the stream, whose mossy banks had not been tampered with—sunbeams dancing on the rippling surface . . .

Rachel stopped, startled. This was not Cole's dream. His was one of immensity, too. Where, then, had such a simplistic idea originated?

In the maze of her twisting and turning thoughts, Rachel suddenly heard a faint scraping sound like wood against wood directly above her head. Before there was time for her feet to respond to the sudden flow of adrenaline of fear, Rachel felt two strong arms snatch her backward. The feel of safety was familiar. Those arms could belong to nobody except Buck—but what had happened?

She was dimly aware of a crash, and his voice in her ear whispering over and over, "Oh, Rachel, Rachel! You could have been killed. I couldn't bear that—oh, Rachel—"

"But what—?" she began, and then saw that a large section

of the scaffolding had fallen from the unfinished building. But what was Buck saying? That the heavy timbers could not have fallen without a push. "Then somebody deliberately—?"

But even as she spoke there was the sound of a breaking twig, followed by a crash in the brush. From the corner of her eye Rachel caught only a glimpse of a man's head bobbing briefly up and down in haste, then disappearing in the green labyrinth of head-high ferns.

Buck made no move to follow. "Walk slowly and don't look back," he whispered in Rachel's ear. "It could be a trick to lure us into ambush—"

Buck linked his arm through hers and began to walk casually toward the village. The grip on her arm was stronger than it would appear from a distance, and there was no choice but to match her gait with his—not that she wanted to linger. She shuddered as they walked with studied calm.

"Who, Buck? How could anybody have timed an accident so well—known I was going to be here? And who would want to? As a matter of fact—" Rachel stopped walking, a motion which caught Buck off-guard and swung him to face her. She looked deeply into his eyes, always kind and now so filled with concern for her safety. "How could *you* have guessed I was here?"

Buck grinned a little sheepishly. "I have been known to stalk ladies I care about—and, oh Rachel, I *do* care about you. Let me take care of you—always!"

Rachel laughed fondly, "Isn't that what you've been doing? Odd that the two men I admire most should offer to protect me from danger!"

Instantly she could have bitten her tongue off. She knew instinctively that she had hurt Buck, and he was the last person in the world she would want to cause to suffer. Before she could put it into words, Buck said in a normal tone, "That is a warning sign."

# 22

## Need for an Answer

Feeling somewhat self-conscious after yesterday's interlude, Rachel returned General Wilkes' wave a little uncertainly. He had stopped at the door of the hotel room serving as a temporary office for Dr. Killjoy—although why he lingered now that Yolanda was back on her feet puzzled Rachel.

She need not have felt uncomfortable. The General, every inch of his giant height a gentleman, would let nothing stand in the way of their warm relationship. Even a flat *no*, disappointing though it might be, would make no difference. Rachel determined, however, that her refusal to his kind proposal would be one of gentle humility. He deserved so much.

General Wilkes consulted his gold pocket watch and hurried Rachel's direction as if to converse with her before an appointment. Rachel turned to thank Buck, but he was gone.

"Has something happened, Rachel? You're so pale."

Rachel could only nod.

Without touching her, the General said softly, "My dear, this is not the time and place. As a matter of fact, I will not repeat my proposal if it distresses you. But surely you must realize you are in danger. Don't you see how much you need someone in whom you can trust completely?"

Numbly, she nodded again. "I'm so grateful," she murmured, knowing that the words were inadequate.

"I urge you to give the matter a great deal of thought. I can wait for—for a short while." His eyes became less serious, and a small smile lifted the corners of his mouth, "I do not demand a June bride. All I ask is that you fully consider the terms."

"Oh, I have—" Rachel felt the words rush out.

He brushed away her words with a gesture of his gloved hand. "Tut, tut, dear Rachel. Do not speak of us in past tense. We shall talk at length later. Think of what happened today—for I am convinced that it had something to do with your safety."

"Some scaffolding fell—that's all."

The General's face paled, but he smiled at her understatement. His clear eyes met Rachel's with such openness that she felt an overwhelming sadness. The Lord would have to help her deal with this. Instead of becoming routine and simple, life was heaping up problem after problem. To resolve one would create another.

Their goodbyes were brief. The General obviously was expected elsewhere, and Rachel had caught sight of Yolanda standing at the door of the Meeting House, pencil and scrap paper in hand.

Then two strange things happened. Rachel waved to Yolanda, but there was no answering wave. She saw then that Yoland's eyes were raised to the door marked "Maynard Killjoy, M.D." And Maynard Killjoy, M.D., Rachel thought wryly, must have been expecting Yolanda because the upstairs window opened, at which time Yolanda waved. Irked for no reason she could explain, Rachel looked over her shoulder curiously to see if the masterful physician would deem it good therapy for the patient if he returned her wave. Apparently he did.

And then to her surprise Rachel saw that General Wilkes

had opened the door of Maynard Killjoy's office. He hesitated before entering, and Rachel had a strange sense that
his military stance lessened and the great shoulders slumped
as he stepped inside. It was the first time she had thought
of him as aging—or ill.

Then she dismissed the thought. There was so much to
do and so much she wanted to discuss with Yolanda. It
seemed so good—so *very* good—to have Yolanda back, for
the two of them to be together. Things could never be the
same for either of them. And yet for a moment, with the
warm sun prickling her skin and turning Rachel's hair to
strands of newly minted copper coins, she could almost
make-believe that the awfulness had never been.

"Yolanda"..."Rachel"...they said simultaneously, both
managing a little laugh. And then they were both talking
at once.

"I was right, wasn't I—about the General's being in love
with you?"..."I thought you were too busy waving to your
friend to notice"..."Rachel, does Buck know?"..."There's
nothing to know!"..."You can't be in love with him—a
man twice your age, no matter how nice—"..."I'm not in
love with anybody, Yo. I never can be again, but I owe him
so much for saving Cole's life—!"..."A life for a life—that's
not the way it works, Rachel."

The conversation was getting nowhere. Or maybe it was.
Rachel had a feeling that getting things out in the open was
good for them both. But there was a more serious matter
she wanted to approach.

"Yolanda—Yo, *listen* to me! You can't listen and talk! Is
there a reason why you continue to see this doctor? How
much do you know about him?"

There was a flash of the old Yolanda in the blue eyes.
"What is it you're asking—*really* asking?"

Rachel laughed. There was no fooling Yolanda. "I
deserved that. I was being devious." She sobered then.

"Yolanda, you said something that disturbed me greatly just after—just after the terrible accident. Something about not trusting in God anymore. As your closest friend, I can't let that happen to you. This doctor—where does he stand?"

Yolanda lifted her chin. "He has asked me to attend church with him Sunday. Does that satisfy you?"

"Not quite, but it's a start. And speaking of starts—"

They busied themselves then with plans for the picnic. The whole community would welcome the opportunity for a big dinner—others having been interrupted by tragedy. Maybe the men would like to play horseshoes while the womenfolk laid out the feast. And the children would never settle for receiving their cards of promotion without "earning" them. There should be a testing. Agreed—and some kind of program. Buck would read the Scripture (Rachel volunteered for him) and Brother Davey might as well be the one to offer the invocation. The Jerico Singers? Yes, Yolanda said—and did Rachel think General Wilkes might wish to speak? She was busy writing on the chalkboard, one of the most valuable items in the last shipment Cole had ordered, and did not turn around when Yolanda asked.

If she had turned, Rachel would have seen the General enter and walk slowly toward her, head down and face drawn with inner pain. Instead, she forgot her misery momentarily and was the teacher once more. Hardly aware that she was smiling, she listed the animals for the children, ranging in grade from Chart Class (those learning their alphabet) to eighth-grade gangling boys and giggling girls. They had enjoyed their "Natural Resources of Oregon" study. Now for a test they could identify the fur-bearing animals which trappers hunted...the animals which furnished food...and the older children could write short essays on "Animals, Friends to Man."

Carefully, in order that the smaller children could read the words, Rachel's slender fingers made graceful circles and stems of manuscript printing: BEAR, DEER, ELK, ANTE-LOPE...MARTEN, RABBIT, SQUIRREL, BEAVER...WOLF, COYOTE, PANTHER, WILDCAT...

She was ready to work on the birds and fish when there was a gentle tap on her shoulder. Involuntarily she jumped. Before she could recover, the General said softly, "I am afraid I need an answer..."

# 23

## Strange Encounter

Rachel looked forward to the end-of-school gathering with mixed emotions. Once she had welcomed community festivities—the fun and fellowship that brought the good people together, binding the ties of Christian love ever tighter. But now? What if history repeated itself and something went wrong tomorrow?

Lordsburg could not withstand another disaster. With so many matters concerning their future in limbo already, how could they handle more? And more was sure to come. It seemed inevitable with Julius Doogan slinking in the wings. And Rachel no longer doubted, in view of the evidence, that it was he who for some reason had set out to destroy her. Undoubtedly he was the agitator among the Indians that General Wilkes had alluded to, and now she was fully convinced that he *had* managed to get into Yolanda's room—probably with the aid of Agnes Grant. The two of them were probably tied together in some kind of strange alliance which was becoming more and more apparent. And goodness alone knew who else might be the man's allies. He was capable of attracting his own kind with his scheming mind. Yes, she must be careful, just as the General and Buck had cautioned. And what was it Yolanda had said that Julius Doogan had wanted of her? Her father's address? What could he possibly want it for?

Rachel laid down the wooden mixing spoon...then

picked it up and continued blending the ingredients of the devil's food cake. She must hurry or the children would be back from practicing the little play that Star had written about Sacajawea (the Birdwoman), who as a stolen Indian maiden from the Shoshone tribe guided the Lewis and Clark expedition up strange mountains and around the rapids of great waters to shallower streams.

As she continued her beating, Rachel's thoughts turned to other concerns. What, she wondered, had prompted General Wilkes to follow her into the Meeting House and begin what sounded like a means of pressing her for an answer to his proposal—only to hurry away? She had not seen him since.

Yes, in a very real sense, she would be relieved when tomorrow was over. She must settle some matters once and for all—and then get on with the city.

●  ●  ●

Friday dawned pristine-clear. Mount Hood, with its perennial collar of snow above a robe made purple by distance, looked so close that the villagers could reach out and touch it. Rachel felt a thrill of pride when she saw the crowd—wasn't this Lordsburg's biggest ever?—gather well before the appointed hour. And she felt an even greater thrill as she watched the eager children perform before their proud parents. In the pleasure of the moment, her apprehensions melted briefly away.

They came back, however, as she watched Yolanda. From behind the improvised curtain where they stood to keep the excited children quiet until they were to perform, Yolanda kept peering anxiously out the window. Try as she would, Rachel was unable to shake off the feeling of deja vu. How well she remembered Yolanda's eyes searching the surrounding hills for Julius Doogan when she had fancied herself in love with him . . . before she knew him for what he was. But she knew now. Surely—? No, it was someone else for whom she was searching. Dr. Killjoy? Probably.

Just where he fitted into Yolanda's life Rachel was not sure, but unless she missed her guess Yolanda was in love with the wrong man again. And she, like the rest of the settlers, could bear no more hurt. Besides, there was another matter that needed investigating where the doctor was concerned. It was imperative that she seek him out. Obviously he was not in the audience—not that she would expect him to bother with common courtesy.

But General Wilkes was speaking now. His face was ashen but his words were eloquent:

> In a sense, Lordsburg symbolizes the state—perhaps even the entire Oregon Territory—in its quiet struggle to combat evil and preserve that which is sacred and holy. Going back to days of the Civil War, I shall always remember that Oregon's principal contribution was that of protecting the frontier against marauding Indians, and the interior from misguided sympathizers. While troops of other states engaged in more glorious activities, perhaps, they were no more essential or arduous in their combat than Oregon folk—then or now, as you march on in the quest of truth . . .

During the rousing applause that followed, Rachel saw that most of the women were leaving to put the finishing touches on the basket dinner. The program was drawing to a close, and with Yolanda's mind a million miles from here it was easy to slip away. She would enter the hotel from the back.

• • •

Dr. Killjoy must have seen her leave the Meeting House. He opened the door to his "office" before she knocked.

"Mrs. Lord!" he exclaimed in mock surprise. "What seems to be the problem?"

*I am not going to let him get to me*, Rachel determined in her mind. *Please, Lord, help me stick by that.*

Biting her lip for control, Rachel said in what she hoped was a normal voice, "I haven't come for help—that is, not medical help, Dr. Killjoy. I need some information regarding some people I love dearly—"

"You know that's impossible!" His voice cut through the air between them. Then, to her surprise, he drew a deep breath and exhaled it in a sign. "Would you care to sit upon my one chair?"

Rachel glanced at the unfinished room and its bleak furnishings. Someday soon it would be better. Meantime, she would thank him to keep a civil tongue. Bridling her own, she sat down on the sagging slipper chair.

"I believe," she said slowly, "that you can answer my questions without violating your code of ethics. You see, they are more personal than professional."

"I will be the judge of that." His tone was noncommittal.

"All right," she found herself blurting out. "Are you in love with Yolanda?"

"Are you in love with my uncle?" he fired back.

"Your *uncle*?" The questions hung there between them. Rachel found herself unable to speak for a moment, but her mind was busy. That this man was General Wilkes' nephew shocked her into silence. Why—why, Maynard Killjoy himself could be responsible for some of the ill happenings, if one let such wild imaginings prevail. Only Rachel determined not to do so. An indictment at this point was unfair.

"Yes, his late wife and my mother were sisters," Dr. Killjoy volunteered.

"Then you are not blood relations—" Rachel began.

"And consequently not his heir—isn't that what you intended saying, Mrs. Lord?" His voice was cynical.

"No—no, I wasn't going to say that at all. I—I have only his welfare at heart. Money means nothing to me. What I wished to find out," she continued in a small voice, "is if he is ill. You see, I care about him very much."

Maynard Killjoy dropped onto the corner of the unmade bed, looking suddenly weary. "You know, you don't strike me as the kind of young lady who would marry a man for his money—and he is wealthy, you know—there is a directness and honesty about you. But, hang it all, that seems to be the story!" He combed his hair with his fingers uncertainly—almost helplessly, Rachel thought.

The pieces were falling together. Maynard Killjoy had three strings in his bow. First, he had come here at the request of General Wilkes to see what he could do for Yolanda. Second, he would assess Lordsburg as a possible place for opening a medical practice. But it occurred to Rachel now that another purpose of his visit was to keep an eye on his uncle. The General must have confided in him—and told him that he intended to ask her to be his wife. That meant he must trust his wife's nephew. That was a recommendation. She would put her other reservations aside—for now.

"Perhaps," she said slowly, "you and I were too hasty in judging each other."

He appraised her coolly, then shrugged. "Perhaps."

With that one word the totally bewildering man jerked himself to his feet and began pacing back and forth in the small room. His walk said he owned the universe. His face said he was lost and confused in it. What was he wrestling with?

At length he paused in front of her. "You know, I've come to admire you," he said grudgingly. "Either you're pure gold or the biggest fake I've yet to meet."

"I'm neither," Rachel assured him. "I'm a normal human

being—not without my share of weaknesses and temptations, but, with God's help, I consider myself above yielding to them—"

"Then you can swear to me that you are not marrying my uncle for his money?"

Rachel met his probing eyes with a look of disarming incredulity, followed by a flaming anger. "How dare you!" She gasped. "I am not on trial! I will swear to nothing at all! But to set the record straight, I will tell you that nothing has been settled between General Wilkes and me. I am only concerned about his welfare. And the *last* thing that concerns me is his money. As a matter of fact, gold has been cruel to me."

Maynard Killjoy held up his hands in surrender. "So I was wrong on all counts. But a man twice your age—an ill man—"

He was obviously abashed. Seizing the advantage, Rachel reminded him of her mission. "Ah, yes, my uncle's health. Yes, I think you are entitled to know. You're aware that he lost a limb during the war?"

Rachel could only shake her head. She would never have guessed by his proud carriage. But that accounted for his failure to kneel with her to hear the children's prayers.

"He is going to lose the other."

"Oh, no!" Rachel cried out in anguish. "Does he know?"

"Only since yesterday—"

So that was what the General meant by saying he needed an early answer. Or was it? He was too gentle, too caring, to allow himself to become a burden. There had to be more.

As if reading the question in her white face, Dr. Killjoy went on in a voice he seemed to be having trouble keeping under control, "There's more. The brave man's without a lung, too—and the other one's going. He's going to die, Rachel—"

"Die—*die*? You can't let him!" Rachel wanted to spring

at him, hurt him as he had hurt her. But something held her back. Perhaps it was the use of her name for the first time. He cared, too . . .

Rachel remembered later that from that point the air was no longer emotionally charged, that the two of them spoke in neutral—even natural—tones, and that the conversation moved along without being pushed.

The doctor was trying to persuade General Wilkes to go to Portland, where there were more experienced doctors. And would Rachel help him—even though the General protested?

Yes, yes, she would do anything. And as for marrying him, although she had planned a *no*, how could she dessert the wonderful man in his hour of need? She owed him so much—

But didn't Rachel realize that the General did not know that he was terminally ill—his time short? A refusal would be far kinder. For her to marry him out of pity would serve to hasten his demise.

Rachel did not know that she was weeping until she felt a large handkerchief, smelling slightly antiseptic, gently blotting away her tears. And then his arms were around her, comforting her, telling her not to be sad . . . that his uncle had lived a productive life . . . and that she had brightened his years . . .

"I will be here to help you deal with all this—"

"And Yolanda—what about Yolanda? Don't toy with her heart. It's too fragile; life is too sacred. I think she's in love with you—we're very close and I can tell."

"I will not break her heart," Maynard Killjoy said.

"But—but—" Rachel raised her face to his. "There are other ways of destroying her. Her faith in God is wavering—"

"*You* will have to take care of that!" he said curtly. "But I promise not to interfere."

# 24

## To Know the Heart

Rachel had hoped to be alone on Saturday. She had a great deal of thinking to do. It was more a matter of *how* to go about what lay ahead than *what* she was going to do about it. But Buck dropped by for their usual Saturday morning coffee while Star was swinging Mary Cole in the rope swing from the ancient oak on the Green. And suddenly Rachel, who was always open and honest with Buck, found herself repeating the entire story. Maybe talking would reorient herself.

In her concentration she did not see the shadow that crossed his face or the little pulse beating in his temple as he stiffened against further hurt. She only heard his voice.

"Do you love either of them?"

"*Either* of them? Whatever are you talking about?"

When Buck spoke again, she was surprised by the urgent vibrancy in his voice. "It is possible that the doctor's in love with you too, Rachel. Sometimes people behave negatively to hide their feelings. But give it some thought."

"It is ridiculous—and I have too much to give thought to already—"

"I know, Darling, I know. And certainly I would do nothing knowingly to add to it." Buck paused as if about to say something more—so characteristic of him lately—then he switched topics. "As a matter of fact, I took a liberty yesterday which I hope is all right, Rachel. The men—the shareholders—wanted a meeting after the program. I looked for you—"

"I was with Dr. Killjoy—I'm sorry."

"I told them that, as of now, you plan to close the mine. You haven't changed your mind?"

Rachel shook her head vigorously. "I *never* will! It would be like desecrating a tomb—" Her voice broke.

Buck reached out an awkward hand. "I feel the same way. When the lawyer comes we will know just how the shares are drawn up, but I think you have the power to do it. And there are profits—dividends—even more gold yet to market—"

"Oh, Buck, I thank you for taking over! Don't ever leave me—I couldn't carry on—"

"Rachel—oh, Rachel, I never will—" Buck made a move to cover the short distance between them at the small table. "Give me a chance to prove myself—"

"As if you haven't already!" she said warmly. What was it in her voice that stopped him? "Without you I will be unable to complete Cole's dream—it's what I live for—"

"Rachel!" Suddenly his voice was hoarse with emotion. "Rachel darling, don't let it become an obsession—"

A knock at the door stopped what he was about to say. "The General is here," he said instead. "He wants to share in the dream too."

The formalities of greeting over, Rachel and General Wilkes sat facing each other. Rachel had offered to take his wide-brimmed felt hat, but the General refused. Now he sat fingering the braid, his eyes studying the handwoven rug.

When he looked up, it was with a gasp of delight. "How angelic you look, my dear—the sun making a halo of your golden hair. And don't thank me—just sit portrait-still a moment—"

Rachel concentrated on her hands. They were smoother

these days, now that she had been inside more. But they would roughen again—and happily so, she thought with a proud little lift of her chin—as soon as she could get on with the work cut out for her here.

At the unconscious jutting out of her chin, General Wilkes smiled pleasantly. "And still independent! What an amazing creature you are—and yet there is a part of you that begs for protection. I must tell you that everything has changed drastically since yesterday. Have you given the matter some thought?"

Rachel could only nod. A wrong gesture which the General misunderstood. "Excellent—then let us be married at once. I want the wedding to be more than a civil ceremony, yet I am sensitive to your needs as well. I know you will wish to avoid some of the frills... I have a special clergyman in mind, one who is seeking a church in the area. You will want Yolanda, and I shall ask James Haute to be my attendant. The Marshal—well, perhaps you knew that he is—well, engaged elsewhere—"

Rachel did not know. And things were moving too fast—in a wrong direction. The walls moved in to close around her, and she found herself gasping for air. What had she done? How had she let this happen? She must put an end to it at once!

"But your nephew—"

Did she imagine that his pale face turned more ashen? Certainly it looked more grim when he interrupted almost rudely—a first for the carefully correct gentleman. "So you know of the relationship? I should have told you—except that things are somewhat strained between Maynard—Dr. Killjoy—and myself. We differ on opinions, suffice it to say. However, I can understand your asking why not have him stand up with me. And I shall answer candidly. He does not approve of my marriage."

"But—but—" Rachel wondered numbly if she was so

impoverished for words that she must repeat the word over and over.

"No, I shall ask Mr. Haute. You see, Rachel dear, I need to outline my new will with him. He is coming Monday, according to his message." The General tapped the top-stitched pocket of his regulation jacket. Rachel, following his fingers with her eyes, saw the corner of a yellow envelope. A telegram!

Rachel's mind became a wheel—whirling . . . whirling . . . pausing at one scene, only to move on before it made sense. The doctor's warning that any sudden discovery could be the end . . . Buck's pointing out that both men were vying for her hand . . . and Buck himself . . . yes, she must see Buck. But what for? This was her problem.

"I need to be alone now," she gasped.

Without a word, the General rose from his chair and took both her hands in his, bending then to kiss her fingertips.

"You have made me a very happy man," he said softly. "You will never regret your decision. Look into my eyes and see the truth there!"

Miserably, Rachel raised her eyes to meet his steady gaze. *Now, now is the time . . . I must speak out . . .*

But something in his face held her back. No longer was it ashen. Color had risen to his cheeks and his eyes were almost feverishly bright. Dr. Killjoy, seeing him now, well might say that his uncle had taken out a new lease on life . . .

• • •

Rachel went about preparing the evening meal in a state of confusion. It was as if she had never seen the kitchen before. Where was the butcher knife? And why on earth did the woodstove smoke when there was no wind? The coffeepot boiled over twice. The venison stew stuck to the dinner pot. And the biscuits, she thought in frustration, looked like burnt offerings!

She was in the midst of trying to clean up the clutter and air out the quarters when Buck returned. He took the mop from her hands, finished the job, and with a sharp look at her drawn face ordered her to sit down.

"The General wants to marry me at once," she blurted out with tears in her voice.

"Marry in haste." He tried to say the words lightly.

". . .and repent at leisure," Rachel finished heavily, and wondered if he heard the heartbreak in her voice. "Buck—"

"Yes, my—" Buck stopped whatever term of endearment he had intended.

"Oh, Buck, what am I going to do?"

Buck tried for detachment and failed. "Knowing you, if you gave your word you are too noble to keep it—"

If they said more, Rachel was unable to remember it. Wasn't he going to try and stop her? On the other hand, why should he? He was the good friend he had always been. He was willing to see through anything that would bring her happiness.

Sleep seemed far away, but so was sound thinking. Rachel was not sure when she dozed, but she must have, because she dreamed a beautiful dream. In it she seemed to sit atop Superstition Mountain watching a scene below. There it was, the cottage she had envisioned in place of the palatial house that Cole had begun. Now it was surrounded by lilacs with two little boys—like rowdy twin angels—playing hide-and-seek among them. There was a lush garden, laid out in rows cross-stitched by tall sunflowers, their tall faces turned obediently to the sun. And the roses—oh, the beautiful roses that surrounded a miniscule bed of herbs! And there, kneeling on a cushion, was the familiar figure of a girl. Rachel strained to see the face, but it—like the sunflowers—was turned to the sun. Then as she loosened the soil around the tender plants, the girl suddenly stopped and loosened her hair as well. It fell in like spun silk about her shoulders—the way Cole liked it. Only it was not Cole who approached. It was Buck! The girl turned, and her face matched the brilliance of the sun. Recognition came then. And with recognition, she was jolted awake. She had seen— why, she had seen *herself*!

• • •

On Sunday Rachel was pleased to see Maynard Killjoy in church with Yolanda. Pleased, too, to see that Yolanda appeared to be at peace. Rachel prayed that Yolanda would find that inner peace with the Lord again—that she would reach out and take the Hand that she knew was still waiting to receive her again. The Lord knew Yolanda's suffering...understood that her new feelings were through no disloyalty to Tim...but, having grieved for him, she was ready to start a new life. Of course He understood! It was He who carried her through the dark tunnel when she could no longer walk. *But, somehow, Lord, it is up to You to make Yolanda see that.*

As she thought on these things, Rachel was totally unaware that she was projecting herself into the picture, tracing a resemblance, even welcoming it. She was too absorbed in Yolanda. And maybe, Aunt Em was to tell her later, 'twas best, "for you'd o'rejected the idee then anyhow!"

At the close of the service, she saw Dr. Killjoy help Yolanda into his shiny black buggy. So they were going riding? Rachel waved upon catching Yolanda's eye, and hoped that they would not venture too far out from the settlement.

Maynard Killjoy looked her direction when Yolanda waved. He gave a little mock salute that could have meant anything, and his face told her nothing.

Pleading a headache—which was more fact than fiction—

Rachel excused herself from the usual basket dinner that followed the worship service. Yes, the children could stay, if they would stay close to Uncle Buck or Aunt Em.

She turned away and was about to go to her quarters when she heard her name spoken in low tones. Aunt Em was the speaker. "She's pale-like and nervous as a cat. Either she a-gonna see Dr. Killjoy or I'll be lookin' into it—"

Buck's voice was too low for her to make out much of what he said. But she heard enough that there was no mistaking his meaning.

". . . wouldn't advise that . . . lots on her mind . . . worried more about her safety . . . Doogan's not squeamish about how he lays hands on the fortune . . ."

Fortune? Julius Doogan was after her money—and Buck knew? Rachel was more confused than ever.

As she took one step toward her temporary home, she caught one more fragment. Yes, Buck was saying, she is strong but with one fatal flaw. "She is prone to put the welfare of others above protecting herself—"

"You hafta stop her, Buck. Don't go 'llowin her t'sacrifice her life to one man's memory—an' another man's needs, them bein' so temporary 'n all—"

Rachel stumbled away. How could they know her heart when she did not know it herself?

She must talk with Maynard Killjoy . . . see if he could accomplish what she could not. Then on with the will . . . and the city. Love—*that* kind of love—was out of the question. *Ever!*

# 25

## Promise and Postponement

The days had stretched their length. The summer solstice was past, but barely. The sun still rose over the mountains to awaken sleepy nightbirds early, reached its zenith at high noon, and took due time tucking its chin behind the seaward hills—blessing the Western world with a long velvet twilight. These intermediate moments between sunset and full darkness were among the countless times that Rachel and Cole had enjoyed together in the Oregon Country—their "time alone in the universe," Cole had called them, Rachel achingly recalled.

At this particular twilight-time (marking the end of her strange day and the pause just before tomorrow's arrival of the lawyer) Rachel put Star and Mary Cole to bed a little early—no easy feat, since they complained that the day still held playtime. Mary Cole whimpered while Star reasoned that even the rabbits knew that. They had come out to play. She pointed a triumphant brown finger at two cottontails kicking up their little feet on the Green. "See, Mother Mine?"

"I see," Rachel smiled, "but they play all night. Birds are smarter. They go to bed early so they can say 'Good morning' to the sun."

The words, plus a bonus bedtime story and two glasses of water, won her point. But Rachel heard their whisperings as she stepped out quietly to enjoy the colorful moment—and be alone in it. There was a distant hoot of a grouse and a closer rhythm of yelps as coyotes gave chase to prey. Then silence. In that vast-as-space moment of mystique, Rachel glanced about at the beginnings of the town. Cole had come so far, but there was so far yet to go. In the purple diffusion of light, the unfinished buildings went slightly out of focus as darkness began to thicken in the trees. Like ghosts one moment, in the next they were transformed by the lens of her eye into a thriving city. But always it would be a city of God, as pure in heart as the laughing waterfalls that bounded down the sheer faces of the canyon cliffs.

The Douglas fir and majestic blue spruce must not be touched. And the wild grapes clinging to their trunks and lower limbs must remain, as well as the *everywhereness* of the wildflowers and the ferny dells. Yes, Lordsburg must stay unspoiled.

Rachel was suddenly startled by a whinny from the stable. *Hannibal!* He had heard her footsteps and recognized her voice...and she had neglected the black stallion so shamefully.

Running lightly, she covered the distance from the Green to his stall. The great animal was pathetically glad to see her, pawing at the earth, demanding his freedom to take her wherever her heart desired...except that she would ride alone now.

"Oh, Hannibal," she whispered softly, "I miss him too. We will go, you and I, just as soon as I finish some work here. Easy, Boy—easy—" she soothed, smoothing the velvety black nose, "I promise to take you to him."

The stallion seemed to understand. Yet he whinnied again—in a gentle, persuasive tone. Was it his way of saying he needed more than she could promise?

"I think I understand," Rachel said in awe. "You need Cole, too."

Hannibal was quiet. Had he heard and understood?

Dusk had fallen. One by one, like stars appearing in the June-bright sky, windows of the village lighted up as doors closed against the night. Inside were families—loving families—safe, secure, comforted by the loving arms of home. These were houses made into homes because they sheltered life—man, his mate, and the echoes of their children's laughter. These were homes that had tasted death, had found it bitter, and then, lifting their arms to heaven in supplication, had found joy again...

Rachel turned sadly. Her house was no longer a home. Without Cole it would never be again. Neither would the new house ever become a home in any sense of the definition. It would have no heart. The near-mansion, as Cole had envisioned it, might have served their purpose well. But without him it was a mocking reminder of her loss. It was too elegant without his dynamic presence and the people he had planned to entertain...too *pretentious*. In fact, she sighed deeply, she would never live in it...so why bother to complete it? She could never occupy it—never, *never*!

Deep in her thoughts, at first she failed to see the long shadow cast in the pool of light spilling from the parlor window of the hotel. So Dr. Killjoy's voice behind her caused her to jump.

"I didn't mean to startle you, Rachel—Mrs. Lord—but, seeing you here—incidentally, weren't you supposed to exercise a little caution?"

"I was about to go inside," Rachel said somewhat stiffly.

"I won't detain you. Coming right to the point," he said, moving closer to make sure they were not overheard, "Were you able to persuade my uncle to go to the Portland facility?"

Trying hard not to let her agitation show, Rachel explained that the conversation never reached that point. Instead, General Wilkes had somehow misunderstood and thought she had accepted his proposal.

"In that case, I would advise letting the matter stand. As I told you, any shock can be his undoing. Would you like to have me try again at making him see how imperative it is for him to seek further evaluation before—before taking a wife?"

His voice was surprisingly kind. Expecting to be scolded, Rachel found herself touched by his change in attitude. When she nodded, she was further surprised that Maynard Killjoy reached out his hands to grip her forearms and draw her closer—but careful that their bodies did not touch. Then abruptly he let her go.

Turning on her heel, Rachel lifted her cotton skirt and began to run across the Green. Halfway, she stopped. Something had caught her eye. There was no motion—just the suggestion of another presence. She turned slowly and, even in the darkness, was able to make out the familiar form of Buck. Of course, he would be looking after her, she thought fondly. Almost—*almost*—Rachel ran back to thank him. Almost, but not quite. Why? She wondered.

# 26

## I Leave to Thee. . .

Rachel entered her quarters and paused before lighting a lamp. She must check on the children, but she needed a moment to collect her thoughts. Dropping onto her small settee, she reached out and found the comforting warmth of Moreover. The faithful Irish wolfhound was like a guard always—and more so if she left the quarters. It was easy to see that he was perplexed by his master's disappearance. Only a loyal servant to Cole, now he became hers. The breed was so intelligent that there was no need to remind him of his charges. Nobody could come within sniffing distance—and Rachel was sure the long nose picked up scents from the neighboring settlements—and hope to leave with all moving parts, should there be any question. The children were his pack.

What a loyal friend, she thought, stroking the silky, gray face. Loyal without question. Without faultfinding or complaining. Yielding, always yielding to her wishes—

Like Buck! Like Buck and Hannibal. Only not like Buck at all. Buck was in a class by himself. She could get no further in her thinking. It became fragmented. Like the day. Like time. Like life itself. . .

Rachel lifted the chimney from the oil-burning lamp in preparation for lighting the wick. Then she paused to listen. Yes, she was sure someone was below, and something told her it was for no good purpose. There was a sibilant sound of whispering. Trying to make no noise, she crept to the window and parted the drapes. A man was moving with the stealthiness of a panther—obviously accustomed to spying. And his conspirator, bent over, was parting the lilac bushes and moving toward the hotel.

Agnes Grant! And the other mystery person? It was . . . it *had* to be Julius Doogan. So the danger, for whatever reason, was real. Rachel wished with all her heart that she had Buck beside her. How glad, how very glad, she would be when tomorrow was finished. At least it might shed some light on matters.

Carefully Rachel closed the drapes and moved away. Her jaw had tightened and the nagging headache that had become so much a part of her recently gave a lightning-quick warning, then settled to a heavy throb in both temples. Like Hannibal, she was alone . . . more alone than she had ever been in her life. This time Cole was not coming back. And yet . . . and yet . . . although she had mourned his death with every fiber of her being—mourned until her tear ducts were dry and there was no blood left in her heart—mourning was such a lonely partner . . .

Frightened by such thoughts and feeling disloyal that she was perhaps thinking dangerously, Rachel ran to Cole's old rocker that had sat idle since the explosion, and with a moan sank into its depths. Afraid of her thoughts, afraid of night stalkings, afraid of tomorrow and the future alone—or, by twist of fate, with General Wilkes—she prayed fervently that her fears would be removed.

For how long she prayed Rachel did not know. She heard the opening and closing of doors. Purple twilight having deepened into moonless dusk, the villagers were coming onto the porches. The evening meal was over. Dishes were scalded and put away. Now, with long sighs and loosened belts, they reclined in well-worn chairs or the old porch swing that added a bit of grandeur to the hotel gallery.

Their presence was comforting, but it was impersonal—not meeting a need that she herself did not understand. And so she prayed on as the basso of the bullfrogs added its deep-throated harmony to the creaking of the chairs and the low murmurings of contentment that spelled out enjoyment of one another's company at the end of a long, hard day.

The longed-for breeze rose, toyed with Rachel's drapes, and then touched its fingers to her burning temples. The headache—and, yes, the heartache—remained. But the fear had subsided. "Thank You, Lord," she whispered, hugging the corduroy cushion to her in relief.

Then her right hand touched something oblong in shape and smooth like...paper. Something left there?

Rachel spent no more time in speculation. Her fingers closed around the object, tracing its shape. She held it tight as, with shaking hands, she lighted the lamp. Without looking she knew what it was. A letter—very long, very fat. It was the letter she had received the day the General's telegram came!

Without bothering to look at the hand-canceled postmark, she knew that it came from Portland. And, just as instinctively, she knew that it came from Cole—mailed, undoubtedly, on his last trip to the city.

Quickly she glanced at the heavy sheaf of papers without reading them. The first line told her what she suspected already. This was her copy of Cole's last will and testament. One phrase told her that: "...being sound of mind..."

Rachel reached instead for the smaller envelope which her husband had enclosed. It was marked simply "Rachel."

*Read*, her mind willed. *No!* Her heart cried out in despair. And, in the gray shade between the two, reasoning told her to wait. For what she did not know. Slowly she opened it.

She must force herself to get her emotions in order. The information might be needed for tomorrow. Rachel wavered. And, at last—seeming to have no will of her own—she began to read:

> *My darling, my darling: I leave my dream in your keeping.* . . (her eyes blurred and she skipped down a few lines). . . *I loved you too long from a distance—which may be the only kind of love men like me can give* . . . *I leave to thee* . . .

And then she could read no more. Folding the letter away, Rachel put it in the little jewel box of her mother's. It would have to wait until she was stronger. She closed the drawer, crawled into bed without removing her clothing, and stared dry-eyed at the dark rafters. *Oh, Cole, why did you go?*

# 27

## Reading of the Will

Rachel awoke with a feeling of excitement. Still in the lap of sleep, there was no accounting for her change in meeting the day. Depression had clouded the morning's glory of late to the point that she expected it. But now she looked out upon the predawn shadows of the mountains as they draped the dewy valley and through half-closed lids saw the miracle spread before her, feeling a stir of joy that neared exhilaration. Still barely visible were the jagged tree-lined peaks rising victoriously into the sky. Soon the stars, dimming even as she watched, would blink out one-by-one and her day would begin.

But for now her heart sang out with the words of Exodus: "In the morning you shall see the glory of the Lord." And for one shining moment Rachel seemed to see His shining face...

Such moments should last forever, she thought tiredly a short time later. Yawning and stretching, she let the dreams of the night fade and the June scene outside her window enlarge as the familiar ache that filled her days returned.

So many things were crowding her mind of late that, Rachel realized with a start, she had neglected Yolanda. Yolanda was well now, she tried to reassure herself, so why all the concern—except the natural longing to see a beloved friend? No, it was more—a feeling that Yolanda needed her.

Somehow she must manage time for her.

And then, as the fiery rim of the sun pushed back the pink curtains of dawn and crested the mountains, Rachel felt a familiar tingling along her spine. It was pleasant, urging her to meet the day with expectancy. But it was at the same time unpleasant in the sense that she knew she must face the unknown. And somehow, although she wondered where such an idea could have originated, Rachel knew that today was to mark the end of life as both of them knew it. Close all other doors, and open the new. To her, and later to Yolanda...

Thoroughly confused, she brushed her hair, braided it, and pinned the golden braids around her head while the sunshine warmed her back. Forcing a smile at her reflection in the cheval mirror, she started to prepare the children's cereal. Then she turned back to the mirror, noting that for the first time in ages life glowed in her like a flickering flame, waiting to be fanned. But even as she watched, it dimmed...

●   ●   ●

General Wilkes had offered to introduce James Haute and leave Rachel alone with him to hear the terms of Cole's will. No, Rachel decided, she preferred to have him with her—and Buck, of course. She needed his presence. Yes, the Meeting House would be fine. How early? Eight would be fine.

Now Rachel lifted the folds of her dark serge skirt above the level of the dew and walked with more serenity than she felt toward the door well ahead of the appointed time. It seemed fitting that she should take a moment to survey the fruits of Cole's labors toward the city.

There were still no sidewalks and no streets as such—just rutted trails and one boardwalk. But roads forked out from the village in every direction, wide and waiting to be finished like the rest of the town. And everywhere she looked the growth was evident. Gone now were the shacks put together with crudely split boards and roofed with canvas from the covered wagons. In their place were well-structured buildings, and she knew that the expansion was plotted and planned.

Rachel opened the door and walked inside. For a moment she stood in the saffron light of the sun sifting through the window panes. And then she walked to the altar and knelt, asking God to sustain her through this ordeal.

Deep in prayer, Rachel was unaware that the door had opened and closed until someone knelt beside her. At first he did not touch her, and Rachel knew that he too was in prayer. *Buck—dear, dear Buck.* She knew even before his large hand reached out to cover her clasped hands.

"Are you up to this, Rachel? I can handle it, you know—"

Rachel shook her head but did not withdraw her hands. She needed his closeness. "I'm all right," she said, "as long as you are beside me."

"I'll be here as long as I am needed."

Buck's simple statement quieted her troubled spirits. Kneeling like this, there was something sacred about the togetherness—something, Rachel thought with a familiar ache, poignantly sweet, akin to her last moments with Cole.

She realized then that Buck had asked her something and that she must ask him to repeat the question. "I'm sorry—"

"I asked if General Wilkes was able to handle your refusal to his proposal—you *did* tell him?"

Rachel hesitated. How could she make him understand? "I didn't tell him, Buck—I mean, I was unable to say no in view of. . .everything. He's ill, and he saved Cole's life—"

"And I didn't—" Buck whispered brokenly.

"Oh, Buck, no!" Gently Rachel laced her fingers through his. "It isn't the same at all—"

Together they shared a short silence. Rachel felt warmth

radiate from Buck's fingertips to her own, then flow into every part of her—loosening knots of tension, dispelling fatigue, blotting out her fears of today's unknown factors.

And then the silence was split by the rumble of carriage wheels, excited squeals of children, and the sound of adult greetings. James Haute had arrived. Their moment was gone.

But it left Rachel with an uneasy feeling of something unfinished. As soon as Buck released her hands, the old fears, misgivings, and loneliness returned. What was the matter with her anyway? It was as if her entire being were undergoing a violent and unexplainable change—and inside her heart was a deep, black hole that fed on stars... destroying everything she loved...no, every*body*...and leaving the world in darkness...

* * *

James Haute appeared to be in his midthirties. Short in stature, his thinness gave him a look of greater height. But the hand that accepted Rachel's proffered one was fine-boned and smooth, speaking of indoor work. His black hair glistened with oil he used for slicking it back for a middle-part. Rachel found herself concentrating on his hair where it curled up on the ends to balance with his waxed mustache that lifted in question marks. But the brown eyes were keen with intelligence, and there was nothing comical in his manner.

Rachel acknowledged the introduction and hoped that it was not raining in Portland—although it usually was. Not in June, he said, as if she should know. So shouldn't they get right to business? The lawyer was unfolding papers without waiting for an answer.

General Wilkes, with his usual military precision, waited until Rachel was seated. Then, carefully, he seated himself across the aisle. Buck sat down in front of her. It was odd that she would notice such minor details yet find it impossible to concentrate in depth on what the man was reading and then commenting on. Business she would leave to Buck. He would understand and interpret for her.

James Haute moved with lightning speed through the formalities preceding the actual terms of "one Colby Lord, deceased." Mrs. Lord did understand, of course, that she and the children inherited the bulk of her husband's estate? She, of course, would be responsible to seeing that "said children shared and shared alike." However (clearing his throat uncomfortably), it seemed, er, "proper" that Buckley Jones (Buckley? Rachel had understood that "Buck" was a short form of the "Buckeye" nickname he had picked up on his trips over the Applegate Trail—then she brought herself back to the reading of the will). . .yes, proper that a *man* be appointed executor. Mrs. Lord *did* understand that women did not usually take part in such matters?

Buck interrupted at that point. "I object to the implication here. Rachel—Mrs. Lord—is perfectly capable of managing her husband's affairs. However, we understand the laws, small as we are here. And, of course, I consider it a privilege to help—*providing*, proper or not, Rachel wishes?"

Rachel bit back the tears. How well Buck understood her need to participate actively—not to be left out or put down by tradition. Aunt Em was right: She was a woman before her time, and (with a lift of her chin) Cole would want their daughters brought up in the same manner. Buck would clear the way.

There was no hesitation in her answer, "Of course, Mr. Jones is to handle the matter," she said with simple dignity.

The lawyer paled, then flushed. He read on determinedly, but Rachel sensed a certain respect, if not admiration, in his tone that had been missing before.

There were considerable funds from the stocks, and more

coming from the unmarketed gold (each of the settlers, as shareholders, would profit to "no small degree"). Then, although there were loans outstanding, there would be ample money to complete the building in progress. Yes, Mrs. Lord was well-provided-for even though she closed the mine—unless—

Suddenly James Haute pushed the papers from him and stood. He seemed about to speak but began pacing back and forth for short distances.

"Now the unpleasant part," he said at last. "As your attorney, I must caution you that certain parties—and I must protect my source—are less than satisfied with the arrangement—"

Buck sprang to his feet. "*Satisfied!* What interest have 'certain parties' in Cole's estate?"

The lawyer hesitated. "I am not at liberty to divulge. You see, sir, said parties have contacted me to represent them in the matter of filing claim against the estate."

"If I may interrupt," General Wilkes said in a quiet voice, but one which carried a near-command, "I should like to point out that it would be unethical for you to represent whoever your other clients may be."

James Haute waved away the possibility that he was not aware. "However, in Mrs. Lord's best interests, I want her to retain my services. You see, sir, this person—and, yes, his followers—are capable of bending the law, which in a sense is on their side. You see, there was a prior claim, it seems, to Blue Bucket Mine..."

At that point Rachel's senses blurred. She was aware of only one thing—and of it she was certain. The man behind this was Julius Doogan. The danger was real, as she had been forewarned.

But what was this Mr. Haute was saying? That the man filing suit had witnesses to a certain "flaw of character" which he was prepared to use against her in court?

Even through the mists of confusion that clouded her mind, Rachel was aware of Buck's anger—something she had never seen before. What was it Aunt Em had said? "You can measure a man's character, Dearie, by th' size o' what makes him mad!" What had she missed that would so arouse his ire?

"Then he's threatening Rachel herself—and perhaps the children! That is an invasion of privacy—it's blackmail!"

"Both," James Haute agreed, snapping his briefcase shut. "He will be trying to make contact—watch her like a hawk!"

"Come out and say it, Haute!" Buck spat out angrily. "It's Doogan—the man who posed as judge, who held Cole—"

"The name doesn't matter. It, too, may be an alias—he has several. And now I shall see about lodging for a couple of days before returning to the city."

Rachel was faintly aware that Buck was steering her to the door and that General Wilkes had detained the lawyer. All else seemed blotted out—except their voices.

Dimly she heard, "But why the rush, General? I will be here tomorrow—"

"Tomorrow could be too late," General Wilkes said softly. "I am in need of two wills—one in case of my survival and the other in case of my demise. Wait? I have waited too long—I should like to return to Portland with you."

# 28

## The Author and Finisher

Yolanda must have felt the same need to see Rachel that Rachel felt to see her. And she was first to arrange a visit.

Rachel caught a glimpse of Yolanda from the corner of her eye. Then, captivated, she turned to look again. The new start of sourdough could wait. Although hers had gone flat, the borrowing from Aunt Em was more an excuse to see her dear friend and to confide in one of those heart-to-heart talks that had begun on the Oregon Trail and continued to endure—and, yes, to check on the antics of Agnes Grant. Supposedly the busybody was lending Aunt Em a hand at the hotel, but Rachel must caution her friend to keep a close watch on her—without letting the woman, or anyone else, know why.

Even as she turned her full attention to Yolanda, Rachel realized that the Galloways were alerted to the possibility of Julius Doogan's possible presence. He alone would be the target of such sharp-tongued phrases as Brother Davey was spitting out: "...get my hands on that bandy-legged coyote...make 'im into fish bait...after I'd ground 'im with my fists!"

And Aunt Em was correcting and scolding gently as always. It was a part of her makeup that endeared her to all. Somehow the older woman managed to miss being comical. And her promptings to her adored "Davey Love" were hardly carping.

"Now, now, David Saul, be rememberin' your callin' calls fer peace with all men—"

"Right, Emmy Gal! But he ain't no man a 'tall—he's a viper, a yeller-bellied viper...and I'll grind 'im with my fists and—"

"Grind 'im with your *heel*'s th' Word...and best you stop grindin' your teeth an' help peelin' th' last o' the summer's apples. Pies t'bake—and Preservin' Day at th' Lees..."

Mention of *Lee* turned Rachel's full attention to Yolanda Lee Norval, who was tethering Tombstone, the family's ancient nag, to the hitching post and waving at the same time. Rachel smiled a heartfelt welcome and ran to meet her.

But somewhere back in her mind she tucked a smile of affection for the Galloways and another for the somewhat amusing sight that Yolanda had made in her grand entrance into the village. Her brilliant auburn hair was bound wisplessly beneath a wide-brimmed straw hat with blue ribbons trailing down the back like a grosgrain waterfall. And she wore the blue cotton skirt with a ruffle that stopped just above her high-topped shoes—both of which she usually reserved for Sunday or a school program.

What, Rachel wondered, was the occasion? And to come riding in astride the old horse...she pulled the corners of her mouth into a disciplined line...no smiling now...

Not that Yolanda would have noticed! At the sound of an upstairs window being opened, she whirled to wave at the man who had saved her life (and captured her heart as well). Yolanda's face, when she turned back to Rachel, absolutely glowed. Add that to the wide-eyed wonderment and the secret was no longer a secret, but open for the world to see.

And her laugh! The sound of Christmas bells had returned to it. But signs were not enough. Before there was time for a greeting, Yolanda burst out with her news.

"Maynard has asked me to marry him!"

"He *what*?"

At Rachel's gasp, Yolanda reached down and snapped a buttercup from its hiding place in the clump of ferns at the bottom of the outside stairs. She nibbled at the stem as the two of them climbed the wooden steps. Her face was partially concealed and Rachel could no longer see it. "You seem surprised—as if—as if—I were making another mistake!"

There was defiance in her voice. But Rachel recognized that the defiance was mixed with anxiety. Yolanda sounded like a child waiting for approval before she is sure she has acted correctly. Dear, sweet, caring...nothing must cloud her skies again. If Maynard Killjoy proved false—

Yolanda's great, dark-fringed eyes were raised to Rachel's now. Rachel met them squarely. And suddenly their arms were about each other.

Both of them were weeping as they entered Rachel's quarters. With their arms still around each other, they dropped onto the small settee.

"Tell me you approve," Yolanda begged.

Rachel laughed in spite of herself. "What I think has nothing to do with it, darling. Oh, Yo, don't you know that all in this world I want for you is your happiness?"

"But you have reservations?" Yolanda was wiping her eyes. "You think a person with such a fine background— oh, Rachel, he's been everywhere and someday we'll go together, he said...Edinburgh was once his home, and he talks about Shakespeare's home—Shakespeare, Shelley—" Yolanda stopped suddenly. "You're right," she said, sobering; "why would he care about a country bumpkin like me—a man who recites Keats—?"

"Does he recite any of the Psalms?" Rachel asked gently. "I don't want to hurt you—"

Yolanda lifted her chin, her eyes sparkling with defiance again. "You're really questioning *me*, aren't you? About my faith in God's caring...well, I still feel that we have to fend for ourselves . . . instead of depending on Him. Where did my childlike faith get me—you—*them*—ANYBODY?"

Rachel winced. By *them* she knew that Yolanda meant the husbands they had sacrificed. The old hurt came back, but she could live with it now. Nothing was in vain.

"Yo—listen to me, darling. This hurt will pass. And whatever happens, you must never surrender to doubts. Together let's go back to the faith of our childhood. *We* may have changed, but *God* hasn't—no, don't interrupt me, please! Remember the old hymn we used to sing together—each trying to outshout the other—'Faith of our Fathers'?"

Yolanda nodded and a tear slid down her cheek. "It's never changed, Yo—not even in your heart. Deep down, it's still there—that same faith that caused Abel to offer a more excellent sacrifice than Cain, that led Noah to build the ark . . . Abraham to sojourn into the strange country in search of a city. These all died in faith, darling—as did (she choked the words) your Tim and my Cole—"

Yolanda's face blanched and then she whispered: "Faith is the substance of things hoped for, the evidence of things not seen."

Joining hands, they sat silently, each in her own prayer. But Rachel knew that something had happened inside the heart of her dearest friend—something wonderful.

"And now," she said brightly, "what was your answer to the rising young doctor?"

Immediately the old Yolanda was back. There was a ripple of laughter. "Oh, Rachel, I'm in love. I'm in *love*. I'm in LOVE!" She paused and then continued as if thinking aloud.

"He wants us to be married at once. There's a clergyman coming, a friend of General Wilkes'. I couldn't bear to have—to have Brother Davey—"

"I understand," Rachel managed to say calmly. But in her heart she wondered why the big rush. And she wished with all her being that she felt no reservations. Why was there any doubt, anyway? He had explained his reasons for being abrupt with her—not that she agreed, but that was beside the point. Was it the fact that he had not revealed his relationship with the General? Neither had the General, and she would trust him with her life. Was it the money and his ugly accusations? To be fair, others would wonder too . . .

Whatever doubts remained, one thing was certain: He had brought new life to Yolanda. She had opened up to his affection like a bud responding to a summer shower. And for that Rachel was grateful to him.

"I'm so happy for you, Yolanda," Rachel said sincerely.

"Oh, I knew you would be!" Yolanda sang out, and then, as if to make sure there was no wall left between them, she dropped her eyes and struggled with the words she said. "You know, I—I must make a confession. Silly as it sounds now, I was jealous of you for a time. I wanted what you had and found it—but it's always you that men adore—"

Rachel tried weakly to protest, but Yolanda blurted out her confession. "Yes, I *was* jealous. I even confronted Maynard with it—we've discussed *everything*—and he said we were both lovely. You're sunshine, he said. And me— I'm moonlight—*romantic*, you know?"

Yes, Rachel knew, but love—what about love?

Yolanda was answering her unvoiced question. "But the *main* difference is that he loves *me!*" The pansy eyes were triumphant. "And I love *him* in a way I never thought possible."

Somehow we've managed to reverse our definition of love, Rachel thought. Once Yolanda argued that love came from a long friendship. That accounted for her frequent postponement of marriage with Timothy Norval. Rachel had held out for the "twinkle of an eye" love that was so all-consuming that it could not be denied. And now here Yolanda had obviously fallen head-over-heels in love with a man who had been a total stranger just a short time ago, while she—

*Yes, Rachel, what about you?* An inner voice prompted. Why, she herself could never fall in love again by any definition.

Suddenly aware that Yolanda was studying her face, Rachel colored. Yolanda's eyes narrowed slightly. "Rachel, I'm sorry—here I am going on and on about my forthcoming marriage while I thoughtlessly ignore the fact that you have had a proposal—"

"It's not the same," Rachel said sadly. She intended to let the matter go at that. Instead she found herself telling Yolanda the whole story, omitting only the scene between herself and Dr. Maynard Killjoy.

The pupils of Yolanda's eyes enlarged. "Rachel," she gasped, "you can't let him go away thinking—believing you'll marry him. And you can't—you just *can't* marry him after what you've *had*! Wait for the real thing again."

"It won't come again," Rachel said with a note of finality in her voice and (without realizing it) a note of determination. "And you're right—certainly I can't marry a fine gentleman out of sympathy or appreciation."

"It would be a counterfeit marriage! What are you going to do to make him understand?"

"I don't know," Rachel said helplessly.

Yolanda bit her lower lip, obviously holding back words she wanted to say. Instead she murmured something about meeting Maynard and was about to leave when she stopped to ask abruptly, "Did you hear from your father?"

"My *father*!" Rachel hand went to her heart. She had forgotten completely that Julius Doogan had coerced Yolanda into letting Templeton Buchanan's address be known. Oh, that Yolanda's father had not stayed in touch with the man with whom he once fished the Atlantic shores!

"Pa had a letter saying something about blood being thicker than water, so he must have heard of your loss—"

"More likely my gain!" Rachel said bitterly. "A gold mine would buy him a lot of rum."

Yolanda was all sympathy. "I shouldn't have mentioned it—yes, I should so you will be forewarned. But maybe he won't come—just—" Yolanda hesitated and then said boldly, "Hold onto your faith!"

"Oh, I'm glad you said that!" Rachel said, planting a warm kiss on Yolanda's cheek. "Let's each think on what the other has said this morning. Promise?"

Yolanda promised. And the two young widows parted.

• • •

On Sunday Yolanda and Maynard came to church. Yolanda was all aglow, but the doctor's face looked drawn, as if he had been struggling with a problem.

Rachel was soon to know what the problem was.

Brother Davey brought his lengthy sermon to an end with an invitation for "all folks out there who ain't never met th' Lord" to meet Him at the altar, adding that "if there's them what's met th' Almighty and fallen away from His ways" to join the "new converts."

The Jericho Singers began humming softly "Just As I Am," and—as if moved by the spirit—Nola Lee went to take her daughter's place at the harpsichord and Yolanda went back to where Maynard Killjoy was seated. She offered him her hand. Together they walked down the aisle and knelt at the altar.

Rachel was too overcome to cry. God had heard her prayers and brought Yolanda home. In that kingdom-come moment, she slipped quietly from the back seat she had occupied and tiptoed outside, unaware that Buck had followed.

Then suddenly his arms were around her and they were sharing the sacred moment. "Oh, Buck," she whispered, "How beautiful—how beautiful!"

The tears flowed then because she had Buck's shoulder to lean on. "They're going to be married, you know—"

Buck said nothing but continued to hold her close to the comforting warmth of his Sunday suitcoat. "I'm happy that Yolanda has found both loves again—only—does it seem too soon?"

"Love can happen like that," Buck said softly into her braids. "It's best that we be still and trust the Author and Finisher of our faith—"

Be still. Yes. Rachel relaxed in his arms.

# 29

<center>~~~~~</center>

# Farewell, My Love!

"Can you catch a glimpse of Lordsburg as it will be?" Rachel asked Buck dreamily as the two of them studied the plans Cole had made and given to Buck for safekeeping.

"Yes—yes, I can." Buck said. "Emigrant families mingling with the earlier settlers here." He smiled. "A regular Tower of Babel."

Rachel hardly heard. She was seeing graveled streets, more boardwalks, the newspaper office, a doctor (of course it had to be Maynard now), the church completed (a cathedral by comparison to the Meeting House used for worship now), and business after business (all law-abiding, in accordance with Cole's will and the convictions of the village folk). *Village folk!* She realized suddenly that they too would be moving, except for the hotel guests. But that was part of the agreement. And she, Rachel realized with a jolt, would be among the movers! Worse, she had no place to go since deciding not to continue with the great house that Cole wanted for her.

At her frown, Buck looked concerned. "Problem?"

Once she would have told him what troubled her, but the atmosphere seemed strained since he had held her in his arms two days go. Something had stirred within her, something she never expected to feel again. . .*something that could not be!*

"Rachel," Buck spoke a little huskily, "I've been giving

151

some thought to building a small cottage on my claim and—"

There was a rap on the door of Rachel's quarters and she rose quickly, relieved somehow—and at the same time disappointed—that Buck had been interrupted.

"General!" Rachel spoke with an enthusiam born of released tension. "Do come in—Buck and I were just finishing."

The two men shook hands and exchanged a few words, and Buck left abruptly. Rachel wished she had not seen his look of hurt.

Shaken by it, she took the General's hat, invited him to be seated, and said she would see if the coffee was still hot. However, before she could turn, General Wilkes had clasped her wrist gently. "No coffee—nothing, my dear. Just sit beside me."

He moved over, making room for her on the settee. Now, now was the time to tell him. But he was speaking.

"I've come to say goodby," he said quietly. "I will be leaving early in the morning. Would that I could take you with me as my wife...but I am afraid that—and the rest of life—must wait for awhile. You see, my dear Rachel, I am afraid I will be unable to fullfill my promises—and I release you—"

"I know," Rachel whispered. "You need not explain—"

"Thank you. And should things go well for me, my offer stands. But until we know (he rose), it is farewell, my love!"

Rachel stood on tiptoe and kissed his wind-weathered cheek, knowing that she would not see him again.

# 30

### ❧❧❧

# County Seat

July brought a burst of heat. Garden flowers wilted under the white-hot sun, except for the hardy zinnias in Aunt Em's rock flowerbeds. The zinnias were as persistent as Rachel. Buck's loyalty and encouragement supported her in the zealous drive to carry on with Cole's dream. *Nothing can stop the two of us*, Rachel kept repeating in her heart, *in following the wishes of the man we both love.*

The men divided their time equally between finishing their own cabins and donating work to Lordsburg's completion. Rachel was happy that the giant oaks refused to be intimidated by the merciless sun. Their mammoth trunks continued to transport minerals and moisture from their strong root system to their splendid leaves, making a cool, green canopy under which the workmen could hammer, saw, plan, and talk.

It was pleasant talk, she noted happily—centered on closure of the mine and eventual disposition of their findings, still carefully stored away. They had accepted Buck's announcement of her decision to close Blue Bucket without derision—thanks to Buck's careful explanation of her feelings and the provisions of Cole's will which shared with them more generously than they had expected. Trust Buck to do all things in keeping with her desires...in reality, *Cole's* desires.

There were times when Rachel felt that she was unable

to go on. But with the vision of a finished city dancing like a mirage before her eyes, with renewed vigor she followed the burning desire that became her master. Lordsburg would never become the capital city as Cole had once dreamed. But, she vowed, it would be a bona fide city, with older buildings finished and reoccupied after their closure during the mining era and new ones mushrooming to expand the perimeter . . . growing, flourishing, and *alive!* That way Cole would achieve a certain immortality . . .

"The church is finished," Buck said with pleasure.

Rachel stood back to admire the shake roof and the belfry crowning the roof and reaching into the sky. The old mission bell looked happy to have found a home again. "It's beautiful," she said in awe. "Now we can take the organ out of storage—"

"But let's not part with the harpsichord. That was in the first wagon train I helped cross the Rockies—and I guess I'm overly sentimental about old things—"

"Yes," Rachel agreed, "it's like an old friend."

"And old friendships are the best. You know, at one time Yolanda's philosophy was that the deepest and longest-lasting love was born of friendship."

Rachel remembered, but she was not to be deterred. Her mind had leaped ahead to new pews for the church . . . perhaps red runners down the aisles . . . and, of course, the new organ. What a touch it would add! Cole had chosen the best—a full-size hardwood instrument of rare quality with a canopy top and a mirror above the keyboard, allowing, he had said with a smile, the organist to watch her hands and at the same time the new hats which the ladies in the congregation were wearing!

Rachel was ecstatic when in late August word came by telegram that Lordsburg had been designated as County Seat.

She had been strolling with Buck on one of the rare

evenings that she allowed herself to be pulled from her notes. Those free times had been highly rewarding, refreshing, and surprising. As she and Buck talked, she learned more and more about him and saw a side not heretofore revealed—his interest in music, for instance. He preferred Bach to Beethoven. Rachel disagreed, and Buck said they would listen to both when his new hand-cranked graphophone came.

"You've ordered us one?" Her surprise was complete—so complete that she failed to notice the *us* of her question.

Star had interrupted and Rachel forgot the incident.

Now, strolling again, Rachel read and reread the telegram, stopping only when she noticed Buck's silence. "Well!" she said a little tartly, "I hope the *Council* is pleased!"

"They will be, Rachel—and so am I. But I am not pleased with—with your driving yourself so hard. It isn't what Cole would have wanted. Oh, Darling, don't let it consume you!"

Rachel was angry—unreasonably so. "I'm cold," she said, although the night was sultry. Turning, she almost ran home.

# 31

## To Rachel with Love

Dried peas were picked, threshed, and sacked—then the beans. Cornstalks, stripped of their ears, were topped for fodder on which the stock and cattle would winter. It was time for "Preservin' Day" at the Lees. There the valley folk for miles around would bring their harvests to a common storehouse to be canned, bottled, dried, and divided equally. But this year Rachel was too busy to go. She had received word that more materials would arrive on the same September day.

"We really should." Buck's words were a mild reprimand—a reprimand missed by Rachel. She only picked up the plurality of his words and was relieved that she would not be left alone in the village.

Now she looked over the fallow fields—row after row, marching along like friendly troops. But her mind's eye saw freshly turned soil, rich and black, and then the endless acres of sun-ripened grain raising its golden beard high, waiting patiently for the sickle. And then spring! Spring, when the village would be finished—unless she decided to expand it. After all, Lordsburg was now the County Seat...

Oregon's representatives, having no choice actually, voted in favor of self-government. The Council of Lordsburg followed suit. It seemed farfetched that the village would boast a courthouse—or did it? they asked at their meetings. With the men home from the mine the sky was the limit.

It was better—and, admittedly, safer—to be shareholders in a growing city than in a mine as ill-fated as Blue Bucket had been. Best be getting a judge and electing a representative to go to Washington.

Yes, the future, once so dark, was beginning to take on brightness. Just look at how far they had come. Why, there was the printing press starting up with a single-sheet weekly publication, *The Bugle Call*...the second lumber mill...and two smithies now. And, as for a doctor, could anybody who had been tended to by Maynard Killjoy question that his prescriptions were kinder to the palate than Aunt Em's concoctions?

When the homesteaders' cabins were chinked in for winter comfort, they volunteered their help and that of their field hands. Once the buildings which were originally under construction were completed, however, they wondered among themselves why Mrs. Lord saw fit to push for spreading out. But she seemed deaf to a breathing spell.

"They've all but broken their backs, Rachel," Buck said kindly, and yet there was a cutting edge of warning to his voice. "They've sawed down the trees and blasted out the stumps—even delved into the kegs of black powder to blow out the boulders. It seems to me that we should call a halt—maybe concentrate on the *quality* instead of expansion—"

The two of them stood in the silence of Lordsburg, the others having gone to the Lees' "Preservin' Day"—all except William Mead and Dr. Killjoy, who said he was expecting mail and would wait for the boat; then he would join Yolanda.

Rachel thought for a few minutes before speaking. She must choose her words well. Actually, she was hurt by Buck's surprising change of attitude. He had led her to believe that he was as eager to carry out Cole's wishes as she was.

When Rachel made no reply, Buck surprised her by

reaching out and laying his hands lightly on her shoulders. Then, without seeming aware of his action, he let his hands slide down her forearms and come to rest on her elbows. There his grip tightened.

He looked searchingly into her eyes. Automatically Rachel stiffened without knowing why. It was not the inherent strength of his face or the strength of his big, square hands. No, they made her feel protected, cared for. It was something more. His mouth, usually humorous and kindly, was set in a straight line. And in his eyes was a compelling look she had not seen before. Something about the look frightened her. She—why, she was seeing a *stranger*.

"Rachel—Rachel darling," he whispered hoarsely, even though there was no audience, "can't you—just for this single moment while we are alone, even without the children, can't you be—well, *you*?"

Something within Rachel stirred again. Something nameless. Something she had thought dead. She found herself wanting to relax against him, to stop struggling, to let him take over her life and just be a part of him—a part she had not been before.

"Yes, the children are with Aunt Em," she found herself murmuring senselessly, "and we are alone—"

With a little groan then, Buck pulled her roughly against him. "Oh, Rachel—tell me—just tell me, what is *your* dream? You don't want the big house, and you're bone-tired. Let me take care of you. Don't you know how much I love you—have always loved you from the moment we met?"

Rachel drew back startled. Buck, their dearest friend, was declaring himself? And she was permitting it? She tore herself away, afraid of her own emotions.

"I was married when you met me," she said more coldly than she intended.

Buck was immediately apologetic. "Oh, I didn't mean that! I would never allow myself to covet another man's wife—

certainly not the wife of my dearest friend. It's one thing for a crow to fly over and quite another to let it nest in my hair."

His misery tore at her being, but Rachel hardened her heart against it. Such talk was disloyal to Cole's memory—disloyal to his dream. "You are a treasured friend—nothing more. No man ever will be. Now, let's get busy or you might as well go ahead to the Lees when Dr. Killjoy goes."

"And leave you alone? You know I won't. You might as well know there have been several unsavory-looking men skulking around. The danger's not over. I will help you, yes, even though I realize now that you are right—you *are* incapable of loving again, just as Dr. Killjoy feared."

"Dr. *Killjoy*!"

"He warned me from the start that the catastrophe had cut a deeper groove into your emotions than Yolanda's. Some of his behavior was aimed at treating the wounds. He knew his uncle planned to—to ask you to share his life, and Maynard's interest was for him."

Buck's face was ashen and his eyes were angry. This Rachel saw from the corner of her eye. And, although her anger matched his own, there was a touch of sadness flowing through her veins. *Things can never be the same between us.*

But back to business. Rachel, looking a little pathetic in her attempts to gain control of the situation, lifted her chin.

"No, I am not going to complete the house. What do you think of converting it into a community center—calling it Lordsburg Inn? There could be appropriate rooms for conducting city affairs, and a large library... we could combine the drawing room and parlor into a hall for entertaining..."

Even the most casual observer would have noticed the fire which rekindled in Rachel's eyes as she talked. The mood between her and Buck had changed. It was as if he no longer stood watching her with fixed eyes, one telltale muscle quivering in his jaw. Rachel was alone, fulfilling her destiny. They would convert the Meeting House into a courthouse, she said. Remodeling. Adding on rooms for caucuses. The logical place for the courthouse was the Village Green, the center of what would become the largest, most thriving city in the Oregon Country. And with the church finished, the building no longer needed to serve that purpose. And Amity was finished—

"Don't you agree? The men wanted a Bachelor Hall, you know . . . well, I'm still opposed, but there can be rooms for privacy in the Inn . . ."

Rachel turned shining eyes to Buck. But Buck no longer stood facing her. He had never walked away from her before. Why now when she needed his approval?

There was no time to concentrate further. Rachel found herself surrounded by supply wagons which, buried in her thoughts, she had failed to hear. The shipment of marble had come, a ragged driver (whose breath reeked of alcohol) told her. Uneasily, she directed that it be unloaded near the Meeting House instead of the site of what was to have been the Lord home. There was more marble at the quarry— and did Mrs. Lord have use of a piano player who could double his responsibilities . . . you know (leeringly), playing in the bar weekdays and at church on Sundays? He could qualify, being a "religious alcoholic" like he was . . .

Rachel told him coldly that there would be no need for his services. There would be no bar in this city. Then, frightened by the ways his eyes traveled the length of her body, then darted along the deserted streets, she hurried to direct the unloading of other merchandise. Buck—where was Buck? Didn't he know she needed him? Frantically she hurried toward the post office, completely unaware that she had turned to Buck instead of Cole's memory for guidance and protection.

She was nearing the hotel when she caught sight of Buck. He was capably assisting the other workers. And for one moment Rachel felt an overwhelming desire to run to him, to pour out her loneliness and her despair—and, yes, to tell him that he meant more to her than she had admitted even to herself. . .

But Willie Mead was coming from the post office. "Mrs. Lord!" he called just as Rachel would have lifted her skirt and run to Buck. "There's mail for you."

Rachel accepted the single letter and would have put it in the pocket of her woolen sweater had the postmark not caught her eyes: Portland. And the return address read "John B. Wilkes, U.S. Cavalry, Ret., Rose Sanatorium."

Rachel felt a chill of apprehension. With trembling fingers she opened the flap.

> To Rachel, With Love: By the time you receive this, I will have gone to my reward. But I cannot leave without telling you how much happiness you have brought into my life—and telling you how gallant and brave you have been as a frontier woman. I would have pursued Cole's dream with you—and yet I beg you to pursue a dream of your own, to be the joyous, fulfilled woman God intends you to be. You need youth, not dead dreams. . .Oh, my darling, be happy—as Cole and I would have you be. Open your eyes to a new spring. . .*Live!*

# 32

## In Loving Memory

Rachel stood for several minutes with the letter pressed against her heart, then (leaving the rest of the supervising to Buck) stumbled to her quarters. There she wept in solitude—more for the world than for herself or the General. He had given the world so much and would keep on giving, she remembered from scanning the remainder of the letter. He was sending the attorney back with the terms of his will—part of his worldly goods left in trust to Rachel for supporting the church and school, another part to his "granddaughters," Star and Mary Cole Lord, and the remainder to his closest surviving relative, Dr. Maynard Killjoy (and his bride-to-be), for their pleasure and security. Mr. Haute would explain the rest, but it was done with love to "all beneficiaries and our loving God."

At last Rachel dried her eyes and sat up, feeling an overwhelming desire to make the too-long-postponed pilgrimage to Superstition Mountain. Some magnetic pull beyond her understanding would wait no longer. She and the children must go. . .

Rachel took a warmer wrap from the one small closet—a soft forest-green cape with a hood—and pulled on woolen gloves. There was an early chill to the air.

Telling herself she would walk, think, and look for other signs of approaching autumn, she soon found herself heading in the general direction of where she had last seen

Buck. If he would saddle Hannibal for her, she could meet the returning wagons at the forks and from there take Star and Mary Cole with her as far as the trail would lead up the mountain. There they could be together, pay tribute to Cole's memory, and pray. There also she could bury in her heart the hurt of her most recent loss, the fatherly figure of her beloved friend, as nature had buried her husband.

But, to Rachel's surprise, it was Maynard Killjoy who emerged from the hotel to meet her. She would have supposed him gone to the Lees long before.

"Rachel," he called. "Wait—I have something to share."

It did not surprise her that he drew a bulky envelope from his coat pocket. "The General—" she began.

Maynard interrupted her. "Yes," he said quietly. "But there's more." Fumbling in his other pocket, he withdrew a yellow envelope edged in black. Nobody needed to tell her. General Wilkes was dead.

"Oh, Maynard—I'm so sorry—" she whispered. "So sorry—"

Rachel reached out and clutched his hand. In response, his arms closed around her in a warm gesture of understanding. There was a tender moment in which the two of them shared a common loss—much like she and Buck had shared when they lost Cole.

"Don't cry, Rachel," Maynard said with surprising gentleness. "We mustn't mourn his passing. It was inevitable—"

But Rachel did cry. She cried hard into the oversized handkerchief Maynard Killjoy offered. "It—it just seems— that I am losing so many I love—"

"We're not losing them, Rachel. Yolanda has taught me that! These bodies of ours are not meant to be permanent places of residence—just inns we occupy until the Lord calls."

As he let her go and wiped away a last tear with his thumb, Rachel felt an odd lift of spirit. Maynard was right: So many people were coming home to God in Lordsburg. And, she added to the thought, Buck was right, too. It was better to keep working on the *quality* of this God-chosen place than to spend so much energy expanding.

It was Maynard who saddled the horses. After he left word with Willie as to his and Mrs. Lord's whereabouts, the two of them rode away together. They talked about the terms of the will as they rode, and Rachel knew that all differences between them were settled once and for all. They were, in a strange sense, "family." And she could not think of a better husband for Yolanda.

It was Maynard who, once they reached the forks, approached the subject of their forthcoming marriage. "I would like your blessing," he ended after saying he was waiting for Yolanda to name the date.

"You have it!" Rachel replied with a vigor that surprised even herself.

# 33

## Old Fears Renewed

Twilight fell without warning—another sign of late fall. Objects lost their background lighting and then their identity. Rachel caught her breath as the blending of fall foliage hung over the mountain trail like an autumn-toned rainbow. Then it too faded. But overhead a thin sickle moon snared in the leafy branches of overhanging trees. There it waited until an invisible wedge of Canadian Honkers crossed over its beams and journeyed on to the southern climes.

*If Buck would speak now...*

But he was silent as they traveled homeward. Halfway down he paused and wordlessly lifted a sleepy Mary Cole from Hannibal's back. "Think you can ride alone, Sweetheart?" he asked Star.

"Yes, Uncle Buck. I will be most careful."

The four of them were bathed in a soft mellow light and Rachel felt as if a bank of angels surrounded them, softly humming a lullaby. Rachel, too, was bathed in a new mood—one somewhere between melancholy and joy. Aunt Em said it was difficult to tell the difference. Maybe. But Rachel sensed for the first time that they were family— *real* family. She bit into the word and found it sweet. If Buck shared the moment of magic or sensed the change in her, he gave no sign.

Had she ever been so tired or depressed? Rachel wondered

as, after Buck tucked the children into bed and took a near-wordless leave, she shucked off her clothes. It was a familiar feeling, she realized as she heated the water for a bath—much akin to the twisting loneliness in her heart each time Cole left her. Maybe the bath would help.

In the wooden tub she lay back and scooted her body as far as its confines allowed. The water caressed her aching limbs, soothed her knotted nerves, and briefly unraveled the sleeves of care. If only she could lie here forever and face no more problems—other than small domestic ones, like deciding on what to bake for the after-church dinner. Was there no peace, no rest, no (as Buck put it) time for just being Rachel?

Toweling off, her body felt refreshed. But the depression and overall weariness of mind lingered. She was lonely—lonely and afraid. Lonely? More than that. She was lonely for Buck. She—why, she was in love with him! Had been for goodness knows how long. And for the first time she felt no guilt . . .just desire that he would ask her to be his wife, let her share his dream—

Startled, Rachel stopped in midthought. She realized then that, selfishly, she had never asked Buckley Jones what his heart's desire might be . . .

• • •

Rachel dozed, only to be awakened by a little noise she was unable to identify. As she crept noiselessly out of bed, Moreover sniffed, then growled at the door.

"No, Boy, you stay here with the children," Rachel whispered as she shrugged into a white flannel robe and knotted the corded belt.

The dog went obediently to lie down beside the bed that Star and Mary Cole occupied as Rachel unbolted the door and slipped quietly into the night. Just what she was looking for she did not know. She only knew she should investigate.

It was difficult to see. Difficult, too, to slip past the bushes that kept catching at her loose robe. She paused several times to listen, aware that when she stopped, so did the sound—whatever it was. Oh, now she knew! It was footsteps on the just-laid boardwalk leading to the hotel. There the gold was stored, and somehow she knew it was the object.

Shadows crisscrossed in the dim light of the setting moon—still shadows made by the trees and shrubs. But one of the shadows was moving...moving toward her! Rachel realized then how very visible the white wrapper made her. Why, she was a perfect target! And what had possessed her to come out here alone? She must manage to get past the shadow and find Buck—

But no. The shadow was too fast. It had lain in wait for one moment, and the next it had taken on substance, and she was at the mercy of a flesh-and-blood man...

Gone were the enemies of weariness, monotony, frustration, heartbreak, and loneliness. She was dealing with a probable assassin—possible battling for her life. And she knew, even before she heard the hateful voice, who the enemy was.

When Rachel would have screamed, a hand slapped across her mouth hard, sending her reeling backward. For one mad moment she hoped to escape, but then a brutal hand gripped her arm, twisting it cruelly.

"Did you think I'd let you get by with it, you scheming, money-mad woman? *Did you?* I should kill you right now and have it done with after all you've stolen from me. But no! That would be too kind. I'm going to release you now and we'll talk. One scream and you're dead!"

Something flashed before Rachel's horrified eyes. A knife! Julius Doogan held a knife and was moving it dangerously near her throat. She dared not move. And gradually the brutal hands relaxed their death-grip.

"What is it you want?" Rachel panted, finding it hard to breathe. "Name it—and go. I can't go on forever like this—with you stalking my every move—"

There was a nasty laugh. "You won't have to. I've come to claim what's rightfully mine."

"Blue Bucket?" she whispered. "You still claim it?"

"Claim it? I *own* it! I've got the right lawyer and the papers—never mind how. And I've got witnesses you'd never dream of. You see, dear sweet Puritan, we'll never have to go to court if you cooperate. If you don't, I'll smear your name—tell the truth about you and that bastard child of ours—"

"What—what are you saying?" Rachel could only gasp.

"Why, that we were lovers before Colby Lord. I *am* Star's father, you know!"

# 34

## Another Wound

In the days that followed, September giving way to October's bright blue weather, Rachel knew that she was behaving strangely. There was too much to sort out as she sought to make sense of the senseless situation for her to see the looks of quiet concern that followed her movements. One thing she knew: She needed someone in whom she could confide. But who? Once upon a time, Buck would have been her unquestionable choice. Now she felt as shy as a maiden with her first beau—uncertain of every move, cautious and on-guard about every word that would give away her feelings. Whatever he had felt for her had cooled, leaving less than they had shared before. Now there was no longer even friendship—at least not the unaffected relationship in which they could be natural and at ease. Oh, what was she going to do in this situation—and all others?

Yolanda was too busy with her courtship to be of sound mind. Besides, Maynard was her constant companion. Who then could help her, advise her, protect her? She tried to dismiss the problem—be it ever so briefly—as she went about taking care of the children and participating in church and community affairs. But it was as persistent as the crabgrass that Aunt Em complained about so much.

Aunt Em! Of course, she must talk to the motherly woman who had taken Rachel to her ample bosom on the Trail as if she were her own daughter. She found Aunt Em in the big kitchen of the hotel making green-tomato mincemeat. Brother Davey was chopping suet and dicing apples. Both were so delighted to see Rachel that she felt shame wash over her at how she had neglected them in her driving pursuit of carrying on with the business of building the city. But the wonderful Galloways were never ones to reprimand. Instead, they opened their arms and Rachel walked into them.

"Now, now, Dearie, Aunt Em here's seein' there's something amiss, and I'd bet an owl's feather it's something to do with you 'n Buck," Aunt Em soothed as she smoothed straying strands of golden hair from Rachel's hot forehead.

"Yes and no—that is—"

"That is, you're wonderin' whether t'be marrin' 'im? Now, you ain't a'gonna find a better man this side o' heaven—Ouch! Emmy Gal, did you hone this knife? Look what I done to my thumb!" Brother Davey had his finger in his mouth and was sucking away. Aunt Em sized up the situation, winked at Rachel, and plunged in before he could continue with the conversation.

"You know, th' Lord never intended woman should be alone—"

"That was *man!*" Brother Davey mumbled, spitting out a minute amount of blood.

Aunt Em pointedly ignored his antics.

"You've had your share o' dark. Nothin' but shadows in your sweet life. But, you know?" The older woman leaned down to whisper, "There cain't be no shadows without light! And Buck—well, now, he's that light—"

Rachel was hardly hearing. Mention of *shadows* brought back the mission at hand. She had come to talk about the appearance of Julius Doogan . . . his threats . . . his false accusations . . . and the equally false witnesses, whoever they were.

But suddenly she *did* hear. The conversation which had

gone astray suddenly penetrated her confused brain, and she heard. Oh, yes, she heard. And what she heard tore her heart out.

"You know, he's leavin', don't you, Dearie—less'n you stop him?"

The heavy lashes that shadowed Rachel's cheeks flew up and she felt the blood siphon from her face—another bead on the string of surprises and heartaches.

"Leaving?" The word wedged in her throat. *Oh, no, Lord!*

Rachel was dimly aware of the spicy smell of the mince-meat now bubbling on the giant wood range...the high-beamed ceiling of the great kitchen...and Aunt Em's bending over to wrap a flannel cloth around her husband's finger. But she was acutely aware that Buck was leaving her...leaving her as Cole had done so many times. But at least Cole had told her where and when. Aunt Em could not bind up this wound...

" 'Nounced it at th' last meetin' o' th' Council—leastwise, said he *might* be goin' this spring. *Woman, have mercy on my thum'* (to Aunt Em)—gonna brang another wagon train—"

Aunt Em gave the bandage an expert twist, securing it tidily and causing Brother Davey to roar with imagined pain. Seizing the moment, she interjected, "*Might be* an' *is* goin' ain't much more akin than a sinner 'n a saint, Dearie! You get stoppin' him—course, that is thinkin' you care? Now me—I steer clear as I can of bein' meddlesome-like, but I'd like you to be prayin' on this—that there's gonna be no marriages in heaven."

"Praise th' Lord!" Brother Davey said then (after one look at his wife's face). "Praise th' Lord Em's fixed my thumb!"

"You're paler'n a bedsheet, Dearie—here, tuck this into that tummy. Better be lookin' after th' inner self before tacklin' any more o' th' world's problems." Aunt Em had placed an enormous wedge of pie on the table and was forcing Rachel into a chair.

Rachel toyed with her fork, then laid it aside. "What it boils down to," she said tonelessly, "is that Buck's leaving without asking—"

Horrified, she caught herself. But there was no way she could retrieve the statement. Any simpleton would know that Buckley Jones did not have to ask permission to go.

"Come right out'n say it. It'll taste better'n that pie what with my blood sacrifice in it'n all—" Brother Davey began. Then, in a meeker tone, "Women ought'en keep books on their men."

"He's not my man!" Rachel said hotly. Wondering why she was so angry, she failed to see the look of understanding that passed between the Galloways.

# 35

## Forced Conspiracy

Rachel stumbled home—and through the next week. She felt more alone than ever before in her life. Some distant part of her was aware of the comings and goings around her. Another part said she must prepare for the opening of school now that crops were harvested and children could attend. But the part of her being once called a *heart* refused to function—to do the bidding of her mind or her body. Buck kept conveniently out of sight. At first she agonized for herself. Then, in a contradictory turnabout, she felt a wash of resentment. He had no right to deny the children his company. How *dare* Mr. Buckley Jones, City Manager! The anger felt refreshing. *Just wait, Mr. Jones!*

But it was she who waited. And before Buck put in another appearance, something so devastating happened that the world turned upside down...and Rachel Lord's life.

She had lain awake most of the night, giving way to more self-pity than she cared to confess, even in her prayers, when suddenly the noise! It was the same noise Rachel had heard before—the stealthy footsteps on the boardwalk. But before she could open the drapes enough to peer into the darkness, she heard voices—voices so far away that she would have to stay very still if they were to be distinguished.

"You'll do as I say—that was the arrangement when I

smuggled you onto Colby Lord's wagon train heading West!"

*Julius Doogan!* He was threatening somebody. Rachel strained to hear who the victim was. And then came the most pitiful cry she had ever heard.

"Please—*please* spare my life! I done all you ask o' me. I spied 'n reported, even when—may th' Good Shepherd rest my soul—some uv it warn't so. I lied—that's what I don fer you...lied to these people who've been th' only friends God ever sent my direction. My own pa beat me black 'n blue...then my ole man done th' same—"

Rachel missed some of the words as they were buried in pitiful sobs of remorse, while she herself was buried in shock. It was *Agnes Grant!* Agnes Grant, who was brought here by that brute whom Brother Davey rightfully called less than human—

"You've never seen a battering, you hag, until I'm through with you!"

There were sounds of a scuffle. With pounding heart, Rachel pondered what to do. Then, mercifully, it was over and the woman was helplessly agreeing to some plan. *Listen...she must listen hard!* She lay rigid, hardly breathing. And then came the words she needed.

"Get inside there! You've got keys to the hotel. *Get the gold!* And don't be trying anything funny unless you want your bones to be picked by the ravens."

Rachel could visualize Mrs. Grant as she fell on her knees to plead for mercy. There was no choice except for her to agree. And then the parting thrust from Julius Doogan: "I'll be waiting in the grove. Do it now—"

"Whatever you say, Mr. Doogan, but—" (waveringly) "this is th' last—"

There was the unmistakable ring of spurs as Julius Doogan's boot was lifted to the face of the cringing woman...a muffled cry of pain...and the sound of retreating footsteps.

Rachel sprang from her bed, bade Moreover watch out for the children, and—tying on her robe as she descended the stairs—ran toward the hotel. The gold must be saved. It belonged to the settlers. But paramount in her mind was the safety of the Galloways. If she could pass the bushes safely—

But she was too late. A muscular hand closed about her throat, choking her. It was a death-grip...but what happened? Suddenly the hand relaxed, and from out of nowhere came a circle of lanterns. Everybody was talking at once, but Rachel was conscious enough to see that Julius Doogan's face was caught and held in the circle of light and that his mouth, once so arrogant and self-assured, now opened and closed foolishly—like a fish jolted out of the water.

Maynard Killjoy was bending over her. *Maynard?* But where...how...what? "Take care of the prisoner!" he ordered, "and leave the patient to me. It's shock, I think, but I want to check the bruise on her head. *Rachel?*"

But it was Buck who was picking her up. She needed to tell him something...but what could it be?

# 36

# Afterglow

The village was left in delicious afterglow. From every direction Rachel was bombarded with discreet whisperings and proud undertones of excitement. They'd caught th' scalawag this time—caught 'im red-handed. Oughta be strung up 'n quartered, he ought! But this was a Zion-like town—law-abidin' 'n bowin' t'th' Higher Authority—so's there wuz jest no choice in th' matter but t'wait fer th' militia 'n th' Marshal. Yessir, U.S. Marshal Hunt himself wuz comin' with all them witnesses concernin' all th' other crimes th' imposter callin' himself "Doogan" had committed from th' Oregon Territory t'th' East Coast...good thing they all knowed t'be on guard like that...elsewise, Miz Lord coulda been hurt. Led 'em right to 'im, she did—her 'n th' Lord, who wuz always on th' side o' righteousness...

Rachel lay still listening. The sleep medicine that Maynard Killjoy forced her to take had no effect on her ears. Her eyes felt leaden and there were little halos of light that kept dancing foolishly around as if playing tag on the beams of the office where Dr. Killjoy had taken her. But certainly her memory was sharp.

Buck had been most contrary about leaving her. "I refuse to go!" he had said when Maynard asked him to leave. "There's something we have to talk about!"

Buck was angry. Actually angry. Funny thing, because Buck was never angry. And, come to think of it, *she* was angry too. But for the life of her Rachel couldn't remember why. Well, the showdown would just have to wait until she knew. Then she and Buck could have it out. So Rachel had feigned sleep...

Again the voices. The story was incoherent. It was incredible. She was not even sure she had the whole thing ironed out because parts kept wrinkling around the edges. But the best she could tell from the snatches of guarded conversation leaking in through the open window, Julius Doogan was in protective custody until a proper judge arrived. James Haute would be coming, along with the party of men, and he had all the proper signatures on the legal claim to Blue Bucket Mine as well as the forged copies. A proper jury, Lordsburg's first, would be selected to try both the man known as Julius Doogan and Agnes Grant. The latter was in reality a victim. But, because of the attempted threat (albeit amateurish at best), she would have to stand trial. Undoubtedly the jury would recommend clemency as she would turn State's evidence. Also, she had played "double agent" and alerted the men that Doogan was in the area. Then it was just possible that she had bungled the break-in purposely, knowing that the noise would awaken the sleeping Galloways.

The only two gray areas had to do with something quite unrelated. Or so it seemed to Rachel. It was Judson Lee's voice, wasn't it, she heard saying that the Reverend Brother Luke Elmo would arrive the same day? Judson, too, who said that she, Rachel, was in for a surprise that would cause a porcupine to be throwing his quills!

It had not mattered when spoken. But, as Rachel's mind cleared of the dancing lights, she was puzzled. However, fatigue had replaced the lights and she could think no more.

Several times she was aware that the doctor checked on her, feeling her pulse in the darkness. And once she heard other footsteps that were familiar. Buck? Yes, she would know that long-strided step—almost pantherlike—that took his tall frame almost soundlessly wherever he chose to go.

But kissing her forehead? He had done it before. Why was this different? Weren't they angry at each other?

She dozed, and when she awoke her mind was clear. The sun was chinning the eastern mountains and the gold flame of October was giving way to the whisper of winter. Now the only real warmth came at noon. Evenings were chilly and something whispered "frost." Soon the vine maples and oaks would be stripped of their leaves and hibernating animals would settle in for their long winter sleep. The time of budding, blossoming, and harvesting had come and gone. There would be rain and more rain before another spring. Spring! And Buck, like the glory of the seasons, would be gone...

Rachel turned her face to the ceiling and wept, not knowing that Buck, like another spring, was just around the corner.

# 37

## Mutual Desires

Rachel was feeling desolate and abandoned when the children came. There was one timid knock, then an excited scream of "Surprise!" And there, to her wondering eyes, appeared what had to be every child (correction: weren't there some new faces?) who made up Amity School! Typically, they all talked at once, like wildflowers vying for greater splendor.

Miss Rachel must get back...Miss Yolanda was ready as soon as (giggle) her honeymoon was over...it had to be before Christmas...remember the program, Miss Rachel? Maybe right after Thanksgiving...unless Miss Rachel was going honeymooning too?

"What in the world gave you such an idea?" Rachel gasped, but the children simply looked at her with round, knowing eyes—reminding Rachel comically of a giant oak laden with see-it-all-say-nothing acorns.

Yes, she promised. *Yes, yes, YES!* Anything to satisfy them and send them on their way. There was something she needed to attend to. *Now!*

Rachel waved them goodbye from the couch she still occupied (against her will, she thought wryly) in Dr. Killjoy's office. Undoubtedly there was a guard standing by. Else who would have admitted the children? She motioned Star and Mary Cole to stay, and they flew to her like homesick angels. Rachel hugged their warm bodies to her, whispering words of love in the language mother and child understand. At length she spoke.

"Do Mother a favor, darlings—"

Anything, they promised. Minutes later they were on their way to get the souvenir box containing Cole's letter. When they returned, they tactfully said that Uncle Buck was just outside the door and was he to come in please? Not now. The two little messengers nodded obediently and tiptoed away.

It was easier to open Cole's letter now, to read its sad-sweet message and fold it away in her heart for safekeeping in that tender chamber where she had placed the memories of Baby Lorraine and her father—after committing their spirits to God. The tender words which once twisted her heart dry of blood now warmed her entire being. God had mercifully healed.

> My darling, my darling: You sacrificed your life for me here. It will be no problem when I am called upon to do the same for you. You will be reading this only after God has summoned me to a Higher Cause, so I can speak truthfully on this paper bridge which brings me back to you. The truth is, my darling, I would never have permitted you to come to the frontier—knowing as I did the hazards you would face if left alone—had I not known of Buck's love for you...that he would care for you and our children...that his heart's desire more nearly paralleled yours than my inspired, but dangerous, calling.... Let him enrich your life, Rachel darling, as you have enriched mine. Be happy in that new life. This is my last request. This is my heart's desire. In Christ, Cole.

Someday she would share the letter with Star and Mary Cole. But for now she folded it reverently and put it back into the camphorwood box. Then she called out, "Come in, Buck!"

For a split second Buck's face frightened her. It was gray and drawn. Worse, it was grim and forbidding. Even as he dropped on his knees beside the couch, the expression did not alter.

"You could have been killed!" he scolded.

"Yes, I could have—with nobody bothering to help. Not when Julius Doogan grabbed me. Not when he threatened me before. Not even before that. You—why, you've made yourself invisible when—when you knew I needed you!"

It felt good to say the words now that Rachel could recall why she was so angry. There was another reason, too, but it was the sin of omission—not commission. If Buckley Jones cared for her, let him speak his piece!

Which he did. But not in the way Rachel expected...

"I've been here all the time, Rachel." His voice was suddenly tired. "I have watched over you and the children even after you made it very clear that you did not welcome my advances."

Rachel failed to hear the last words. Her mind had stuck on Buck's claim to have been available for Star and Mary Cole. "What do you mean you've watched over the children? You have neglected them—probably broken their hearts—"

At that Buck broke into unexpected laughter. "*Me? I* have neglected them? Where have you been except burying yourself in drawings—devoting yourself entirely to the building instead of your family? Yes, for the most part they have been with me. I took them out to my homestead, showed them the kind of cottage I wanted to build for—for a wife and some little girls. Star loved it, called it a 'Gingerbread House'—"

"They never told me," Rachel said weakly.

Buck drew a deep breath. "There was never time. And, for the records, Rachel, Star has recreated pictures of her natural parents which will refute Doogan's nasty claims of parenthood. The beautiful, dark-haired woman you have wondered about was her mother—Spanish, of course, and killed in the Indian raid on some nameless wagon train. The child finally opened up to me—told me how her natural father had fled on foot, leaving her dying...sounds like something Doogan would do all right...but the pictures bear no resemblance to Doogan. And besides, her natural father was killed by the same tribe. One drawing was of the fatal arrow...shot in the back as he fled the scene.

Rachel was too overcome to speak. There was a thick silence in which she could hear Buck's labored breathing. At last he spoke.

"So I guess my work here is finished. I think you know what my plans are. You've made the town an idol like gold and—"

"But—"

Buck raised a hand, his face grim again. "I am tired, Rachel, so tired. I simply cannot go on wrestling with a shadow—sparring with the memory of a best friend, a friend who, in your memory, will never grow old—"

"But I don't mind growing old!"

"Neither do I—with the woman I love beside me. But I can't ask you to wipe out the past—"

"I can't, but I don't want to live in it, Buck—not anymore. I thought you'd never let me get in a word."

To her embarrassment Rachel burst into tears. "All I ever wanted was a simple cottage—"

Buck's arms reached out uncertainly. "You mean—you mean—?" His tender eyes were searching hers.

"I mean," Rachel said boldly, "that I love you, too."

His arms came down around her then. Tight. Protective.

Loving. *And for always.*

"A small yard, fenced from the deer" (Buck kissed her forehead, the tip of her nose, her hair), "flowers...a cat that purrs beside a crackling fire...you'd settle for *that?*" His voice was hoarse with hope.

"No," she said with mock severity. "Not just that. There must be room for the two daughters you love so much... and two boy-angels...and maybe a litter of kittens in the spring—"

Buck drowned out the last words with a kiss, knowing that two very small dreams would enlarge into one big enough to hold all the desires of their hearts. "Love is greater than our human hearts can envision, Lord," he whispered. "But by Your grace Rachel and I will catch glimpses of it each day..."

Then to Rachel: "Yolanda wants a double wedding— Thanksgiving?"

Rachel tried to pull away. "Why, you bluffer! You planned it all the time! And the children knew! Oh, Buck darling—"

# 38

## Praise the Lord!

Buck took over from there as far as business went. James Haute brought the promised papers and everything was settled in the presence of the other men at the Meeting House. A last piece of business, the trial of Julius Doogan and Agnes Grant, took place there as well—before the Meeting House would become officially the Court House of Lordsburg.

Rachel was spared from attending the trial. Buck reported that it went well—and exactly as expected. Doogan, escorted by the militia, was en route to the Capitol, sentenced to hard labor for enough years that they would undoubtedly outlast him. Mrs. Grant had asked permission to leave. She had had enough of the "wild West" and was remorseful about the torment she had caused.

Rachel listened raptly to Buck's words, then—thinking he was finished—she hurried to tell him that she and Yolanda had come up with a plan for the wedding. It was a little doubtful in a way, but it just might work. Neither wanted a big to-do. Understandable, Buck nodded. And they didn't want Brother Davey to be hurt—but? Yes, Buck understood that this too would stir the ashes of sadness. So why not keep the wedding plans secret, and then—at the close of the Thanksgiving service, when the new minister invited those who willed to come to the altar— the four of them would go (six, really)? Wouldn't it be nice if Brother Davey gave Rachel away as Judson Lee would be giving Yolanda?

Did she imagine it, or did a flicker of a frown cross Buck's brow? Rachel was too happy to give it a second thought. She was going on about the big dinner afterward—just a *natural* time for offering praise. When she glanced at Buck's face again, all signs of a frown—if indeed there had been any—were gone. All she read there was love, a whole world of love.

•  •  •

The church smelled of chrysanthemums mingled with woodsmoke and boiling coffee . . . wafting through the open windows to reveal a faultlessly blue sky. The Jericho Singers sent praises to the high-arched beams, and Aunt Em (who, like Yolanda's parents, had to be taken into confidence) filled in for Yolanda at the new organ, playing loudly if not well. And, to everyone's surprise, she had her hair crimped! Surely that would alert the audience to something.

But as the Reverend Luke Elmo rose to deliver his first sermon in the new church, all eyes turned to him, little knowing that a wedding feast was in the offing.

Inside Rachel's quarters, the two brides lingered a moment—not uncertainly, and not for effect, but more for one last moment's privacy and to make sure they would be compelled to occupy the back pew, thereby arousing no suspicion. It was a wonderful prelude—this time of together-ness in which each young woman looked for and found happiness in the face of the other. Rachel fastened a last button at the neck of Yolanda's velvet suit, its purple tones making her eyes into twin violets. Then she turned around to let Yolanda secure the crushed velour cinch-belt in back of her willow-green crepe. "You glow, you absolutely glow!" a misty-eyed Yolanda said as she turned Rachel back to face her and patted a stray curl into her burnished braids. "But if you could have one tiny wish more—just one, Rachel—what would it be?"

Nothing, absolutely nothing—everything was perfect, but now they must go. Yet, her lifelong friend was not to be deterred. Wouldn't she like—deep down, *wouldn't* she?—to have some blood kin present?

Rachel's heart began to thud unmercifully as the awful possibility came...splitting the universe...sending the eternal sky down around her feet in dangerous blue shards...

"*My father*," she gasped. "Oh, Yo, you couldn't—"

"*I* didn't. *He* did—Julius did." Yolanda was miserable. "He—he bought him off—paid his way here—bribed him into testifying against you. But, Rachel, your father couldn't do it—said he didn't have the stomach for it. He made an awful scene in the courtroom—you know that Celtic temper our fathers share! He pounced on Julius Doogan and would have choked him out of his misery if Pa hadn't told him the jackal wasn't worth dirtying his hands for—oh, say I'm forgiven—"

The area where the sky had been was pitch black. Rachel squeezed her eyes shut against the darkness that threatened to envelop her. "It isn't your fault," she heard herself saying as if from a long distance away. "But where has he been?"

Yolanda embraced her as if she were glass. "At our house, darling—fishing with Pa. And would you believe not a drop of rum? He's going back, Rachel, and was afraid to see you—"

"My father isn't afraid of the devil himself!" The blackness had turned dove-gray. Rachel's anger was bringing her senses back. She remembered Buck's trying to warn her.

"Then you'll see him—let him-uh, fulfill a dream—give

you away?" Yolanda was pleading like a wayward child.

Rachel's vision cleared. "This," she said, raising her chin in the old Rachel Buchanan Lord fashion, "is the city of forgiveness. I have no choice. As for giving me away—that's better than auctioning me off, I guess."

And, suddenly, for no earthly reason at all—and every reason that is holy—the two of them burst into laughter . . .

Outside, Buck and Maynard (white of face but adoring of eye) waited nervously. A look of understanding passed between them all as they hurried into the church. In the back pew, reserved for them by a discreet Abe Lee, sat Templeton Buchanan, looking strangely alone and pathetic . . . and surely he had shrunk in size. Without hesitation, Rachel eased herself into the space beside him. She heard him let out a trembling breath and noted thankfully that, while it smelled of his pipe, there was not a hint of rum. She acknowledged his presence with a flicker of a smile, as she would have greeted a stranger—which he was. There could never be affection between them, Rachel acknowledged, but there need no longer be enmity. How good it felt to be free of that! *What a terrible burden hatred can be, Lord,* she thought. And then she concentrated on the sermon.

Reverend Elmo (the clergyman General Wilkes had invited and soon to become the beloved "Reverend" in Lordsburg) could not have done better. "Hear this, O church!" He prefaced each statement, and the air was rich with *amens* before he made it. His manner was evangelical, with his bare-of-hair head bobbing up and down for emphasis but his gentle manner molding him into the likeness of a prophet. The multitudes were enthralled. And then he drew to a close.

> We are in a time of waiting. We wait here for
> a second coming, when old things will be made

new—a new earth where peace and justice will reign. But, hear this, O church (*Amen! AMEN!*): We do not wait with idle hands. We can light God's lanterns in our hearts—as I invite each of you to do *now*!

Aunt Em began to play softly. And softly, then rising to a rafter-ringing crescendo, the congregation joined in:

"We're march-ing to Zi-on,
Beau-ti-ful, beau-ti-ful Zi-on,
We're marching upward to Zi-on,
The beau-ti-ful ci-ty of God!"

During the last stanza, the wedding party walked slowly down the red-carpeted aisle to meet the astonished Reverend: Rachel on the arm of a near-strutting Templeton Buchanan...Yolanda on the arm of an equally proud Judson Lee...Buck carrying Mary Cole (her hair in Goldilocks ringlets) and leading Star, who carried an armful of colored leaves and wore the face of a sun-tanned angel...followed by Doctor Killjoy, who looked as if he need a tonic!

*But what was this?* Rachel wondered, glancing from the corner of her eye to see Brother Davey leading none other than Agnes Grant. It *was* Agnes, wasn't it? Agnes with her hair poufed out and square bangs across her forehead? What on earth...but Buck was slipping a plain gold ring on her finger above the beautifully set diamond that Cole had given her and Buck had insisted remain there...she was being kissed soundly, as was Yolanda, so they must have taken their vows together...this was no time to think on Brother Davey's schemes.

The new families made their way back down the aisle. And all the people shouted, "Amen! *Praise the Lord!*"

But Brother Davey and Mrs. Grant remained. At the door, Rachel's father squeezed her hand. "Be happy, Girl!" He said huskily, then made his way back to the altar.

# 39

## Unending Spring

Wrapped in a shawl of happiness, Rachel could accept with humor the astounding news of her father's marriage to Agnes Grant. Aunt Em had brought a coffee cake after the men went, in company with the neighbors, to work on the cottage Buck had begun.

Templeton and Agnes had gone back East immediately afterward, Aunt Em said as, with her back to Rachel, she sliced the cake and pulled the coffeepot close to the front of the woodstove where the fire was hotter. "She's gonna be preparin' 'im for Armageddon—you know, make 'im into a real Christian soldier."

"That will take some doing!" Rachel said. And then the two of them enjoyed a comfortable silence before Rachel told her good news. Just a suspicion, mind you, but—

"Praise be, Dearie! Mum's the word, but I can get sewin'!"

• • •

The dormant season Rachel had dreaded was the most wonderful time of her life. She, like the earth, was waiting... Soon a million bulbs would spear the earth and songbirds would lace the air...by then she would feel movement—the same movement that made the tight-fisted buds into blossoms. Then she would tell...

Meantime, the Joneses moved into their "Gingerbread

House." Yolanda and Maynard chose to remain closer to the village in order for the doctor to be near his patients. But that was only a stone's toss across the babbling brook, and Buck, bless him, had built a quaint little footbridge to span the stream. Both families took their rightful place in the community, but the young wives found plenty of time to talk together at the large new Amity School. And each suspected the other had a secret—a secret too sacred to share until they were sure. And then it must first be shared with their husbands...

Winter came, bringing long, lovely evenings beside the crackling fire that Buck had dreamed of. He spent hours talking with Rachel, planning their future, and sharing every detail of his day. But somehow he left a wide margin of time for being with Star and Mary Cole, taking them on long winter walks, listening to their chatter, and doing something mysterious that the children called their "secret mission."

Try as she would, Rachel could get no satisfactory answer. The three of them made up a game that confused more than enlightened her—a song, really, that sent them into fits of laughter.

"We have a secret, just we three," they all sang. Then each took a separate part: "Daddy," "Mary Cole," "and Star, that's me!"

Rachel heard the pandemonium of hammers and saws in Buck's workshop. The secret mission was noisy enough, she thought drowsily as she dozed in front of the fire. She hardly awakened when Buck came in to add another log and tuck a blanket snugly around her feet. She was sound asleep as he brushed the top of her head tenderly with warm lips and whispered, "What makes you think one cradle will be enough? Star says your prayers have been heard and God has both hands full shaping those boy-angels you ordered!"

The drifts of crimson leaves gave way to drifts of pristine snow, dotted here and there with red berries and rabbit tracks, and then at length the snowdrops. There were days when the winds howled down the gorge to poke at the eaves...then howled away, leaving behind polished blue skies. On those days Rachel's spirits soared. Then came the chill-gray days of drizzle when her spirits plummeted. The rains came down heavy and driven hard by the east winds, which whined like some malevolent beast lost in the forests around them. But through it all, there was a deep peace in Rachel's heart such as she had never known before—a different kind of happiness that told her these periods would pass. Meantime, she had her family—her wonderful, incredible family. Truly God was good...

In February the Chinook winds came, melting the snow early and sending a premature spring. The hills sang with its glory. Old-timers said there had never been such a spring. And something premature stirred beneath Rachel's heart. Her secret refused to wait. Like spring, the event came prematurely.

Buck was cutting wood the Saturday she felt life unexpectedly, so she sent Star and Mary Cole for Aunt Em. "I— I'm scared—" Rachel whispered.

"No reason t'be, Dearie," Aunt Em said reassuringly as she lifted a trained ear from Rachel's middle. "It's just that you're eatin' for three!"

*Twins!* At her round-eyed disbelief, the motherly woman nodded. "Time's come you best be checkin' in with Maynard."

"I wish everybody could be this happy," Rachel murmured as Aunt Em buttoned a heavy coat around her even though the March sun was warm. She stopped and placed a restraining hand on Aunt Em's workworn one. "I was thinking I wish my mother were here—and somehow my thoughts went to Father. How—what part did Brother

Davey play in that wedding?"

Aunt Em laughed heartily. "Why, he up 'n married 'em—even gave 'em a blessing, sayin' they deserved each other!"

The three lives were sound as a dollar, Maynard Killjoy said, and it was anybody's guess which the stork would visit first—her or Yolanda.

It was Rachel. The babies bounced into the world at the end of June—early, but "healthy as piglets 'n twice as noisy," Aunt Em proclaimed. Dr. Killjoy agreed with pride.

"Twins—I can't believe it!" Rachel said to a beaming Buck.

"Why not, Mother Mine? Did you not ask expecting to receive?" *Oh, Star, you Miracle Child!*

Rachel and Buck looked at each other with brimming eyes. Then Mary Cole ran between them. "One mine. One sisder's."

Brother Davey picked up one of the babies in each arm in spite of Aunt Em's scoldings. "More alike than two peas in a pod," he said. "Gotta tie me a white string 'round David here's leg t'tell 'im from Saul—but (yanking at his side-whiskers) problem's gonna be which is got th' string!"

They tucked the babies into their twin cradles and quietly tiptoed out, dragging two reluctant little girls into the kitchen for cookies and hot cocoa.

Rachel and Buck looked at each other with stars in their eyes. The whole world was transformed.

*What a wonderful, wonderful marriage!* their eyes said—solid as the Rock upon which the growing city was founded. In that magical moment Rachel felt her whole life parade before her, and she was thankful for all who had crossed its twisting, gloom-filled trails. Those trails—and the people who traveled with her—had led her to the *now* of things, as God in His goodness had known they would from the beginning....